Section G, the top-secret security unit of United Planets, had a special problem on their hands with the situation on Firenze. And for that special problem, they gathered together the most unusual squad in Section G's unusual history. It included:

A research biologist who could bend steel bars like rubber bands—

A middle-aged lady with total *total* recall—

An interplanetary cowboy whose bullwhip was deadlier than a ray gun—

A brazen young lady acrobat who looked like an eight-year-old kid—

A mild young man who never lost a bet in his life—

And the best pickpocket that ever lived.

But Firenze with its CODE DUELLO was to prove a match for the lot of them!

CODE DUELLO

MACK REYNOLDS

WILDSIDE PRESS

PART ONE

I

IRENE KASANSKY said, "He's expecting you. Watch out. The jetsam is flying today." She did things to the bank of orderboxes she had on her desk, even as she clipped out her words. Her deft hands flew, pressing buttons, flicking switches.

Sid Jakes grinned at her. "I've never seen the day," he said, "when you didn't think the jetsam was flying. I hate to say this, Irene, but I think you're a fake. I think you like it here at Section G."

She glared at him.

Lee Chang Chu, who stood next to the assistant Section G head, said, "Irene is the most efficient colleague we have."

Irene snorted and snapped into an orderbox: "Well, find him, then!" She flicked it off and glared up at Lee Chang, standing there hardly five feet tall and very antique Oriental in her *cheongsam* dress. "Let me tell you, Goody Two Shoes, my resignation is in. This efficient colleague has had it. I'm transfering to Statistics."

Sid chuckled over his shoulder even as he led the way to the door to the sanctum sanctorium beyond. "That'll be a neat trick to pull off," he said. "The Old Man wouldn't let you go if the Director of the Commissariat himself was silly enough to want you."

The ultra-secretary glowered at him, but was forced to direct her attention to her chattering orderboxes.

Sid Jakes held open the door for Lee Chang, taking her slim figure in appreciatively, as she tripped through in the ages-old quick shuffle of the Chinese woman.

"Lee Chang," he said, "why don't you marry me? I'm handsome, reasonably young, of charming disposition, am an incredibly competent lover, and have excellent prospects, if our good commissioner will ever drop dead." He hurried ahead of her to deal with the next door.

She cocked her head to one side slightly and thought about it. She said briskly, "Several reasons, Citizen Jakes."

"I can't imagine what they could be."

"Well, though I'm highly flattered by the proposal, I

5

suspect that you're ulcer-prone, in spite of your surface elan. Besides, I doubt if Commissioner Metaxa plans on dropping dead in the immediate future. But, above all, you're already married."

"Um." He made a wry face. "That's true, that's true, but we could always elope to the planet Saudi." He had a finger on the door screen now, activating it, and standing so that the occupant of the office beyond could see him.

"Saudi?" Her voice, as always was a tinkle. It would be a perceptive observer who could suspect that Lee Chang Chu was one of the most efficient supervisors in the cloak and dagger Section G of the Bureau of Investigation, Department of Justice, Commissariat of Interplanetary Affairs.

The door smoothed open and Sid Jakes grinned, even as he politely motioned her to precede him. "Saudi. The planet Saudi. Polygamy," he said.

Ross Metaxa, rumpled of clothes as ever, sat behind his littered desk. He was slightly red of eye, sour of mien and gave a first impression of either too little sleep, or too much bottle belting the night previous.

Before Sid Jakes could get Lee Chang settled into a chair, the Commissioner of Section G growled, "What is a Special Talents class?" He reached into a desk drawer and came up with a squat bottle and three small glasses. "Denebian tequila?" he said, gesturing an invitation with the brown bottle.

Lee Chang Chu shuddered a polite negation.

Sid Jakes said, "I'm much too young, Chief."

Lee Chang said, "It's a project of mine, Commissioner. After all, you put me in charge of recruiting new agents."

He glared at her. Ross Metaxa was the only person in Section G who would have dreamed of glaring at the tiny Chinese. He picked up a report from the mess on his desk, laid it down again and thumped it with the back of his hand.

"Agents, agents! Section G agents, the toughest operatives in United Planets. It takes years to locate a prospect, more years to train one. You're an old hand, Chu; I thought I could trust you with this. In the field, you're as good a supervisor as we have. And in the past you've field trained some of our best. Ronny Bronston, for example." He looked at his assistant, perched on the side of his superior's desk. "How is Bronston?"

"Oh, Ronny'll be all right. You can't crisp him."

"You can evidently come mighty close. How is he?"

"Still unconscious."

6

Metaxa made a face. He looked back at Lee Chang, who was demurely maintaining her peace. "What's this about sending an eight-year-old girl to Falange?"

Sid Jakes laughed. "Chief, you misread that report. Helen just *looks* like an eight-year-old. She's in her mid-twenties."

"How can anybody who looks like an eight-year-old child be a Section G operative? What's this other supposed agent? A Cordon Bleu chef. If this Tri-Di photo with his dossier means anything at all, he looks like a roly-poly middle-aged man. And this . . ."

Lee Chang said mildly, "The point is, Commissioner, they cleaned up the Falange mess. A mess that had cost us three men, experienced agents, before they took over."

Metaxa looked at her blankly, looked back at the report. He poured himself another of the fiery Denebian tequilas and tossed it back. "How could they possibly have?"

Lee Chang came gracefully to her feet. "I suggest we go to the gym. At this time of the day, most of the class is exercising . . . or practicing their special talents."

Ross Metaxa glared at her again, then growled into his orderbox, "Irene, can I be spared for fifteen minutes?"

Sid Jakes and Lee Chang failed to make out the reply, but Metaxa turned the glare from the Chinese girl to the box. "Oh, is that so?" he snapped. "Well, you're fired." He came to his feet and lumbered around the desk, heading for the door. "I don't know why I put up with that woman."

Sid Jakes came to his own feet, to follow. He chuckled. "You put up with her, Chief, because she knows more about the workings of Section G than the three of us, here, put together."

Metaxa snorted.

The Commissioner of Section G stared about him in disbelief. The hall was a madhouse.

Up near the ceiling, a small child was doing things on a trapeze that should have been impossible. Over near one wall, a stocky, not to say plump, man was swinging a shovel around and around his head. Suddenly, he let go and the shovel spun over and over, finally to smash, blade first, into the bull's-eye of what Metaxa could now see was a target, some thirty feet away. Near another wall, a dark complected, serious looking worthy was snapping a bullwhip of the type that could sometimes be seen in Old West historical fiction Tri-Di shows.

Lee Chang, who was leading the way, came up to a

7

dignified man whose huge size was mollified by the anachronistic pince-nez glasses he wore, and his air of the scholarly. He was watching the child trapeze artist. At his feet was the largest dumbbell the Commissioner had ever seen.

"Special talents?" Ross Metaxa blurted, in disgust. His eyes went around the room. "*These* are the agents you've been recruiting for my department?"

Sid Jakes chuckled.

"Shut up, you laughing hyena," Metaxa snapped. "With this Dawnworlds crisis on our hands, we're shorter of trained agents than Section G has ever been, and you come up with this gang of freaks." He glanced at a plain-looking middle-aged woman who looked back at him mildly.

Lee Chang said, "Martha Lorans. She has total recall. With Martha along, a troupe assigned to some emergency can set down on a planet without any records whatsoever on their persons. No matter what data they need for the job, they can carry it in her head."

She indicated the large scholar. "That is Dr. Dorn M. Horsten, top-notch research algae specialist. He has a hobby that is a personal entertainment. Since boyhood he's amused himself with weight lifting and pretzel-tying—using one-inch mild steel bars for pretzels. He is actually one of the strongest human beings in United Planets. His home world helps: it's a one point four G planet. A very nice, soft-spoken gentleman, conspicuous at every unicellular biology meeting for his brilliant mind. Naturally, nobody notices he has muscles, and can do things that any other human being finds impossible."

Ross Metaxa grunted. He said, "What's that fellow doing?"

"Zorro Juarez? He comes from Vacamundo, settled by Argentines. They specialize in raising the best cattle and horses in the confederation, breed them to order to meet the local conditions pertaining on the worlds that desire such animals. The national sport is the use of the bullwhip. Have you ever seen a twenty-foot bullwhip artist perform, Commissioner? Zorro can make old William Tell look very amateurish. He could quarter the apple on the boy's head and peel one half of it in the bargain."

Metaxa said, "Confound it, what good does a bullwhip artist do in this day and age, and among Section G operatives?"

Lee Chang's voice was sweet. "Among other things, it is a most deadly weapon and involves no electronic gadgetry, metal parts, or anything else detectable by search devices."

8

The head of her department grunted and marched across the room to a somewhat colorless looking young man who had been practicing, rather ineptly, at the quick draw.

"How about you?" Metaxa snapped.

The young man—he couldn't have been more than in his mid-twenties—looked up with an air of apology. "I'm lucky," he said.

Ross Metaxa was bleak. "And I'm Rossie, but just to keep things in perspective, I think you'd better call me Commissioner Metaxa, and the hell with the nicknames. I meant what's your so-called special talent?"

"That's what I meant. I'm lucky."

Section G's ultimate head looked at him for a long empty moment. Then he turned his eyes to Lee Chang Chu, in silence.

The diminutive Chinese girl tinkled laughter. "This is Jerry Rhodes, Commissioner. He is quite correct. His special talent is that he is lucky."

Ross Metaxa closed his tired, moist eyes and muttered something inwardly. He opened them again to glare.

Jerry Rhodes cleared his throat, the apology still there. "I don't pretend to explain it."

"I'll bet you don't," Metaxa said. "Show me."

Rhodes thought for a moment. He said, "There is an element I should mention. My own fortunes have to be involved."

"What is that supposed to mean?"

The colorless young man fished in a pocket. "Here is a coin. You know what a coin is?"

"Yes," Metaxa said. "I know what a coin is. In fact, they still use them on various of the less progressive worlds. Listen, Rhodes, or whatever your name is, start off on the basis that I'm not stupid. I didn't get to be Commissioner of Section G by being stupid."

Rhodes said, "Yes, sir. This is an old coin going back to United States days." He looked at it. "Sorry, France."

"All right, all right, a coin."

"Very well. I will wager you a hundred interplanetary credits that if I flick this coin into the air it will come down with the head on top."

Metaxa looked at him. "Very well, flick the coin. I suppose there's some rhyme or reason to this."

Rhodes flicked the coin high. When it bounced to the floor he didn't bother to look. He held out his hand. "You owe me one hundred credits. Will you document it so that I may credit my account?"

Metaxa looked at Lee Chang in irritation. "Anybody could flip a coin and win. A fifty-fifty chance. What's lucky about that?"

"That comes next," Rhodes said gently. "This time I will wager you the same amount that I can flip it heads three times in a row."

Metaxa blinked. "You're on."

Heads. Heads. Heads.

Rhodes said, "You owe me two hundred credits. The next bet is another hundred that I can flip it five times in a row heads—or tails for that matter. You call it."

Metaxa was staring by now. "Let me see that damned coin! What bet comes after that?"

"That I can flip it ten times in a row," Rhodes said. "I seldom manage to cozen anybody into that. Are you game?"

"Yes, but not everybody's!" Metaxa spun back to Lee Chang and Sid Jakes. He pointed to another of the room's occupants. "What does he do?"

Sid answered him this times. "That's George Killmer, Licensed Orbit Computer. A ballistics specialist. He does celestial mechanics problems like solving the equations of motion of planetary systems as an off-hand job when somebody brings in a set of observations on some new system. His main work is computing interstellar flight paths for commercial and military ships, and as such he can go just about anywhere among the settled worlds without anyone thinking of him as a possible agent."

"What's that got to do with Section G?" Metaxa asked. "What's his so-called special talent?"

Sid said, grinning, "He's the best pickpocket Lee Chang was able to locate by going through the files of every planet whose police cooperate with Inter-Planet-Pol. He's probably the best pickpocket who ever lived. Imagine. Almost three thousand planets in U.P. with socioeconomic systems that have crime, and each with an average population of about two billion. And he's the best pickpocket of all."

Ross Metaxa closed his eyes in pain.

When he opened them again, it was to stare at Lee Chang. "Look," he said. "I assume you're not trying deliberately to sabotage Section G. You've been dedicated too long for that. But when I gave you the job of recruiting new agents, I didn't expect you to wind up with a bevy of pickpockets, shovel throwers and . . . and lucky coin flippers. All this is out of the question, understand? We'll go back to our old system."

Lee Chang was shaking her head. "We haven't the time,

10

Commissioner Metaxa. And you know it. We need new agents, fast. We haven't the time to seek out the young men from all over United Planets who are potential Section G operatives, and we haven't got five years for training them. In the past year, this department has had more work than we had in the last ten."

"Do you think I am unfamiliar with that!"

She said, persuasively, "The need to push, prod, pry the member worlds of United Planets into progress is more pressing than ever. And nine out of ten of them resent— or would if they knew what we were about—such pressures on our part. Man will cling, suicidally, to such institutions as religion, political systems, socioeconomic systems, racial beliefs, no matter how much they may be standing in the way of progress. In trying to change such institutions, we've lost a score of experienced agents in the past few months."

His eyes hadn't lost their anger. "You think you know this any better than I do? But I need agents, not freaks."

"You need people who will bring results, Commmissioner. I am combing United Planets to locate them. People with special talents who also have man's dream." She pursed her small mouth in a moue of defiance.

Ross Metaxa pointed over at Jerry Rhodes, who had resumed his miserable attempts to jerk a heavy Model H gun from the holster he had under his left arm.

"What good would that clod do, if he came up against one of the strong-arm bully-boys on the planet Goshen? He'd be crisped before he could get his shooter out. And by the way he handles it, even if he did get it out, he'd probably shoot off his own foot."

"Not with his luck," Sid Jakes said.

Metaxa scoffed. "I suppose you think he could gamble a Goshen pistolero's shooter away from him by matching coins."

Lee Chang said, "We have already had one of our special talents troupes succeed on an assignment. I suggest you give another group a job and see how they work out. If they don't, very well, Commissioner, then you've made your point. Meanwhile, of course, we are also recruiting in the old manner."

The Section G head hesitated.

"How can you lose?" Sid Jakes said humorously. "Put up or shut up, Chief."

Metaxa cast his eyes upward, in search of divine guidance. "Surrounded by stutes," he muttered. Then, to Lee Chang, "You're on. Anything to bring you to your senses." He thought about it. "There's a situation brewing on Fi-

11

renze. The type of job any troupe of competent Section G operatives should be able to handle. Very well, round up four of these miracles of yours and send them to my office."

He turned and marched off, still muttering.

Sid Jakes grinned down at Lee Chang Chu. "Okay, he's tossed you the whistle; let's see how you blow it."

She bit her lower lip thoughtfully, and looked around the hall at her protégés.

They were seated before his desk in a row. Ross Metaxa couldn't keep his eyes from the seeming eight-year-old girl in her pretty little pink party dress and with the pink hair ribbon in her pretty blonde hair which came down to her shoulders in a style of yesteryear.

He rapped, "Are you sure you're twenty-five years old?"

Helen, who had a red ball in her right hand, jumped to the floor, and, bouncing the toy, skipped around the desk singing in a childish treble, "Three little girls in blue, tra la, three little girls in blue." It couldn't have been more charming.

The Commissioner of Section G was in no humor to be charmed. When she sidled up to him to whisper in his ear, he began to growl at her.

She whispered, a lisp in her voice, "You should never ask a lady her age, but it's twenty-six, not twenty-five." Even as she whispered, her tiny child hands twisted the red ball which fell away into halves revealing a hollow center. Quickly deft, she scooped the small hypo-gun from its concealment and ground it into his side.

"Three little girls in blue, *tra la*," she sneered nastily.

The other three present were laughing.

Dr. Dorn Horsten said, "Thank the Holy Ultimate that she's on our side."

"All right, all right," Metaxa said. "The point's made. I suppose your makeup is a natural for eavesdropping and such." He shook his head as she returned to her chair. "It's just that . . ." He let the sentence fade away and looked at the others thus far silent, two special talents operatives.

The one Lee Chang Chu had pointed out earlier as Zorro Juarez, the bullwhip artist from the planet Vacamundo, was a handsome man in the Latin tradition, evidently on the dour and quiet side by nature. He sat fiddling with an object that looked like a cross between a swagger stick and a foot and a half of sawed-off broomhandle. It seemed to be of highly decorated leather.

Metaxa said, "Lee Chang has evidently seen your whip demonstrations. It all sounds very well, but where's the whip?"

Zorro Juarez said, "Wrapped around my waist."

Metaxa snorted. "Not exactly a weapon you could get into action in a hurry."

Zorro had been pounding his leather baton in the palm of his left hand. Suddenly—he must have touched a stud, or something—a section of plastic thong shot out from the end of that baton, which now proved to be the whip handle. He flicked it once and it snaked, to gently pluck out from the Commissioner's breast pocket, the stylo he kept there. Another twist of wrist and the stylo was in the hand of Zorro Juarez. He tossed it on the desk.

"I say, that's a new one," Dorn Horsten said enthusiastically.

Zorro said, even as he touched the stud again, "We all carry them on Vacamundo." The plastic thong disappeared back into the handle.

Metaxa snorted. His eyes went to the fourth member of the party. Jerry Rhodes was slumped in his chair, in an easy-going attitude. His face was pleasantly vacant, almost to the point of being inane.

"I suppose you're going along to bring everybody luck," Metaxa said.

Jerry shrugged amiably. "It doesn't work that way, sir. My luck is only for me. *I* have to be involved."

Metaxa stared at him. "Look, if you're so lucky, why don't you go to the planet Vegas, or one of the other worlds where they have free enterprise, and such things as gambling? You could clean up."

Jerry nodded, agreeably. "Actually, I'm persona non grata on Vegas. But that's not the only thing. You see, you don't have any particular need for money when you're completely lucky. You get everything you need."

"How?"

"Well—" Rhodes hesitated. "Somehow. You never know."

Ross Metaxa grunted, as though in despair. He fished absently in his desk and emerged with his squat brown bottle and several glasses. He said, as though not expecting an affirmative answer. "Would anybody like to try this Denebian tequila?"

"Bit early for me," Horsten murmured politely. The others except Helen, had evidently heard of Metaxa's tequila; they shook their heads, even as the Commissioner poured one of the glasses full.

Helen beat her superior to it. The drink went down as though it was fruit juice. "Um," she said. "Smooth." She put the glass back.

"Smooth?" Metaxa said blankly. He looked at the brown bottle. "That's the first time anybody called it that." He looked at the seeming child, in her party dress, and shaking his head, he evidently decided against his own drink, as though already his senses were betraying him.

He said, "Look, I'm feeling less optimistic about this assignment by the minute, but let's go. Have any of you ever heard of a planet named Firenze?"

Dorn Horsten said slowly, "I attended a conference on the phylum *Thallophyta* there, some years ago. Although at the time I wasn't particularly interested in her institutions, it seemed a moderately progressive world."

"Not progressive enough. Firenze is a comparatively recently colonized planet. Most of the population came from Avalon, which in turn had been settled from Italy. Firenze, in a way, is still a frontier world and one would expect a wonderful atmosphere for the competent to develop. Unfortunately, it hadn't worked out that way."

"And," Helen prompted, serious now, her voice adult, "our job will be to overthrow the politico-economic system and get things underway?"

But Ross Metaxa was scowling denial. "No. To the contrary. The First Signore and his government have been plagued by an underground for decades. An underground so insidious that the measures that have had to be taken to contain it are what are holding up proper development. The planet can't get underway because of the necessity to fight these subversives."

Horsten pushed his pince-nez glasses back onto the bridge of his nose in consideration. "We have a Section G representative there?"

"We did until recently. An old hand named Bulchand. He was challenged by a Florentine and shot."

The four of them looked at him.

Ross Metaxa shifted in his chair. "I mentioned that it was a frontier world. They built up a system of self-defense —or perhaps I should say offense, unrivaled, so far as I can think, since the frontier days of the old United States. Do you remember the saying, *All men are created equal, Samuel Colt made 'em that way?*"

Zorro Juarez said, "You mean they all go armed?"

"I suppose so. A Florentine gentleman is always ready
14

to defend his honor. Evidently, *always*. It leads to some strange complications. In politics, for instance."

Jerry Rhodes said, "How does that follow?"

His superior twisted his less than handsome face. "Ordinarily, the only citizens not eligible to be called out, under their Code Duello, are the First Signore and his Council of Nine. However, no one is exempt during elections. No full citizens, that is; evidently, criminals and lower elements in general are not considered *honorable* enough to come under the code."

Jerry Rhodes said, "You mean that even during the heat of a political campaign these, uh, Florentines, challenge each other to duels, if they're, uh, slighted?"

"Evidently. It's one of the reasons we've had such a time keeping our agents on the planet. Anyone not up on the niceties of their Code Duello winds up getting challenged before the week is out. And, of course, even a Section G agent can't win all the time."

Zorro Juarez said slowly, "It seems to me that when election day rolled around, and the office of First Signore was up for grabs, it would be a matter of the quickest draw, or the best shot, winding up Chief of State."

"You have said it," Metaxa said dryly.

"And you mean we're supporting such a system?" Helen demanded.

Metaxa looked at her. "Don't read more into Section G than is to be found. We're interested in pushing progress. What socioeconomic system, religion or any other institution a planet might have is not our business *if it works*. Firenze is doing fine except for these damn subversives who are continually keeping the place in an uproar."

He looked from one to the other of the four. "For some reason, the Firenze authorities don't seem to be able to crack the underground. Possibly their police methods are inadequate. Very well"—his voice turned insinuating—"you supposedly have special talents. Use them."

II

IRENE KASANSKY, as always, briskly efficient, had arranged their cover.

Helen and Dorn Horsten were easy enough. She was to be his daughter. He was the noted algae specialist, making a tour of the member planets of United Planets, coordinating the most recent developments in the field. While on Firenze he would visit the larger universities.

15

Helen had looked at him and snorted, "Daddy."

Jerry Rhodes said, "If you were only six inches taller, we could do you up like a mopsy and you could go as my mistress."

She glared at him. "If I was six inches taller, I'd clobber you. In fact, I'm thinking of doing it anyway."

Dorn Horsten chuckled. "I'll never get used to it," he said.

She turned her glare on her pseudo-parent. "What's so funny, you overgrown ox?"

"All right, all right," Irene said. She looked at Zorro, twisted her mouth, looked down at the report on him once again. "You'll go as a representative of the cattle industry of your home planet. You'll attempt to sign up some of the Firenze entrepreneurs to import and breed cattle. On these free enterprise planets, especially, real beef, there's always a luxury market for such things as real beef. It's a status symbol."

Zorro had nodded. "Should be easy enough."

Irene Kasansky turned her eyes to Jerry Rhodes, who, after his little verbal bout with Helen, had lapsed back into easy-going bemusement. She said, "What excuse could you possibly have for going to a frontier world such as Firenze?"

He thought about that. Finally, "For fun?"

She didn't bother to answer. She looked down at the dossier on him. "Where did Supervisor Chu ever locate you?" she muttered.

"At a race track."

She looked up at him and he shifted uncomfortably in his chair. He said, as though in apology, "I had just bet on a horse."

All had their eyes on him now.

He cleared his throat and said, as though this explained all, "It broke its leg."

No one said anything.

He said, "However, it won."

"It *won?*" Zorro blurted. "You just said it broke its leg."

"Well, yes, but you see, well, worse things happened to the other horses and jockeys. It was, well, sort of a mess there at the end. But my horse, well, kind of limped over the finish line."

"Don't tell me any more," Irene Kasansky said. "I don't want to hear it. How is this? You're a rich young nincompoop from the planet Catalina. They're taxing your family too much in building that Welfare State of theirs. So you're coming to Firenze to look into the possibilities of transferring your father's variable capital to that frontier world. No, mother's would be better; a father wouldn't leave it in your hands."

Jerry nodded, evidently not displeased by the implication. "Sort of a playboy, eh?"

Helen snorted contempt.

Irene thought about it. "I suppose you could handle that sort of cover. All right, a playboy, a kind of ne'er-do-well." She became brisk again. "I'll have Wardrobe and the others start working on it all. Be ready to be lobbed over to New Albuquerque Spaceport on the shuttle by Monday morning."

Their information on the subversive organization which was keeping Firenze in a state of dither was minimal. In fact, the agent who had been killed there had been due to make a lengthy report immediately before his demise. The report hadn't been forthcoming, and this was one of the first matters Sid Jakes had suggested they check.

Not knowing what facilities the underground organization might have available, they had decided to take maximum security measures themselves, to the point of pretending on the space freighter *Half Moon* not to have known each other, previous to embarking.

They went through the motions of meeting, somewhat stiffly at first. Went through the pretense of Jerry and Zorro reacting negatively to each other. Went to the pretense of Helen getting a childish crush on Zorro.

Only when there were none of the ship's officers in the lounge did they relax to the point of discussing the ramifications of the assignment.

On the third day out, Earth time, Dr. Horsten sat characteristically in a comfort chair, scanning a tape, oblivious to all. Helen had wriggled herself up onto Zorro's lap. Jerry Rhodes had taken on the Second Officer, a burly and surly spaceman, at battle chess. The Second, Helmut Brinker by name, had made the mistake of insisting on stiff wagers, and was finding satisfaction in the fact that obviously his opponent hadn't the advantage of long years of time killing, whilst off watch, devoted to the game.

Jerry, dressed in his foppish Catalina playboy garb, couldn't have cared less, on the face of it, but his men were in precipitate retreat before the onslaught of four of Brinker's tanks.

At the crucial moment, the ship gave an unprecedented lurch and the pieces on the board scrambled. The Second goggled at the disaster. He looked up at the door, toward

17

the ship's bridge, shook his head unbelievingly, stared down at the mess again. He looked up at Jerry accusingly, but then shook his head again.

"It was a sure thing," he said. "And that's the second time."

Jerry said mildly, "The first time, you knocked them over yourself with your sleeve. This time I was just about to counterattack."

The Second glared. "You didn't have a chance. I think I could reconstruct the game."

Jerry said sadly, "It's not the bet, it's the principle of the thing. I'm sure I couldn't reconstruct it, and I doubt if you could."

Helmut came to his feet, poorly suppressed rage obvious. Without another word, he stomped from the lounge.

Zorro said to Helen, "Look. You better get off my lap."

"Why, Uncle Zorro, whyever for?" She looked into his face, in childish innocence.

"Get off my lap, you little witch. Maybe to that burro Brinker you look like a little girl, but I know better."

Jerry said, "Hey, Helen, you can sit on my lap if you want."

She snorted at him, even as she jumped to the floor. She went over to where Jerry was setting up the board again and stood there, her tiny fists on her hips.

"How'd you do that?" she demanded.

"Do what?"

"Twice, when he had you clobbered, right when you didn't have a move to your name, all the pieces fell off."

"Just luck, I guess."

"Just luck my foot." She hopped up on the chair the Second Officer had vacated. "Listen, how do you explain it?"

He put down the pawn he had in his hand and thought about that. "Well, I have one theory."

Horsten looked up from his tape. "I'd like to hear it."

Zorro said, "Me too."

Jerry said, "Well, it's just luck."

The other three grunted in unison.

Helen sneered at him. "Oh, great. Now we understnad the whole thing. However, when we sit down to eat, all the steaks are tough except yours. How come?"

"Luck," Jerry said, his face serious.

Helen snorted disgust.

"No, I mean it," he insisted. "There is luck, you know. Some people are luckier than others."

Dorn Horsten pushed his pince-nez glasses back higher on the bridge of his nose and said, "As a scientist, I have never seen data on the hypothesis."

Jerry Rhodes fished a coin from his pocket. "You've heard of the Laws of Chance?"

"So-called." Horsten nodded.

"All right. Now suppose I flip this coin of mine a hundred times. What happens?"

Zorro, his dark, handsome face interested, supplied the answer. "It comes up fifty times heads and fifty times tails, by the Laws of Chance."

"On an *average*," Jerry said. "But suppose you have a hundred men flipping coins. Out of them, some will flip, say, forty-five heads and fifty-five tails. That doesn't conflict with averages, since some of the others, say will come up with forty-five tails and fifty-five heads. The Laws of Chance are still working."

"What are you getting at?" Helen demanded.

Jerry went on, a sort of dogged element in his argument. "Suppose, instead of a hundred men flipping coins, you have a billion men. Okay, now still not upsetting the Laws of Chance, you might well come up with a few of them flipping one hundred straight heads, and no tails at all. It would be balanced, of course, by others doing the exact opposite."

He looked around at them. "You see what I'm driving at?"

"No," Helen said flatly.

"Well," Jerry said. "That's how it is with luck. Most people average out. That is, good and bad luck balance for them. One day, they're lucky and find a valuable ring, or win at the races, or whatever. The next day, they lose something or have a setback of some type. It all averages out. Good luck and bad."

Dorn Horsten was scowling at him. "Go on."

"Well, it's like flipping the coins. The Laws of Chance aren't disturbed by the fact that some people are luckier than others. You know very well, from your own experience, that some people go through life as though the road had been paved to their particular specifications. Another has such lousy luck that he'll break his arm picking his nose."

Zorro laughed sourly at that.

Helen said, "Okay, what's all this got to do with you?"

Jerry held up his two hands as though all was explained. "There are more than a trillion persons now living on some

19

three thousand United Planets worlds. It all averages out, but some have good luck, some have bad luck. In that whole number is the one person who has the best luck of all."

They looked at him.

"Me."

Dorn Horsten slumped back into his chair, a wry expression on his face.

Helen snarled in disgust, "Yeah, but it could switch at any time, and you'd start flipping tails, you silly jerk."

"No, it won't."

"Why?"

"Because I'm lucky."

Zorro cleared his throat. "Look," he said. "Not to change the subject, but now we're alone I'd like to bring up something."

"Please do," Helen said, looking her disgust at Jerry Rhodes, who shrugged apologetically.

Zorro Juarez said, "This is my first assignment for Section G and Supervisor Lee Chang Chu has sent me out on it before I got a lot of the orientation agents usually have. I know our department is awfully hush-hush, but, purely in the name of effectiveness on my part, I think I ought to be checked out on a couple of points."

"Such as what, Zorro?" Horsten said.

"Well, what's all this about the Dawnworld planets? I know that the *raison d'être* of Section G is to spur progress on all the member worlds of United Planets, so that when the human race finally confronts intelligent alien life—if ever—it will be as strong as possible."

"Well, that's it, friend," Helen told him, her voice dead serious. "The time has come. We're confronting it. And, frankly, the race isn't ready."

Zorro scowled at her. "You mean these Dawnworld planets I've heard rumors about support an intelligent alien life form?"

"Not exactly," Horsten said. "You're wrong on two counts, or, at least, Helen is. One, we're not confronting them. We're desperately avoiding them. We're not ready even to attempt communication. They're so pathetically in advance of our technology that our scientists boggle. For instance, they have fusion reactors, in short, unlimited power. They also have matter converters. They can, literally, convert any form of matter into any other form they wish." He dropped the bombshell. "However, the term intelligent-alien-life-form does not apply. Evidently, they aren't intelligent."

20

Zorro bug-eyed him.

The doctor shook his head. "I reacted the same way, when Sid Jakes revealed the existence of the Dawnworlds to me. However, given enough time even a very low level mentality could develop an advanced technology. For that matter, some life forms do fantastically well with no intelligence at all—as we know it. Take the Earth insect, the ant. They accomplish wonderful engineering feats, they milk their own type cattle, they store up provisions for the future, they conduct military actions; I could go on. But is the individual ant intelligent?"

The younger man was shaking his head. "But matter converters . . ."

Dorn Horsten shrugged. "There's another possible explanation. On his way toward Utopia, man needed intelligence. He needed it in the caves to survive, he needed it in the days of early breakthroughs such as fire, agriculture, the domestication of animals. He needed it all through such socioeconomic systems as primitive communism, chattel slavery, feudalism, capitalism. The race was escaping from the bonds of nature, trying to achieve food, clothing, shelter and the other necessities, and finally the luxuries, for all. But when Utopia is achieved? When we have matter converters and unlimited power? Ah, then possibly the need changes. Intelligence might even become a disadvantage. The gifted are inclined to rock the boat, and, given Utopia, the average man, the ungifted, doesn't want the boat rocked."

Jerry Rhodes said, "I see what you mean. They could attempt to breed the gifted out of the race."

"That's one possible explanation." Horsten shrugged. "However, whatever the explanation, there the Dawnmen are. And far, far in advance of the human race."

Zorro puzzled along with it. "If they're not intelligent, a really sharp human should be able to take them."

"How do you mean?" Jerry said.

Zorro looked over at him. "Well, for instance, if we could get hold of that method of constructing fusion reactors, or a sample of one of those matter converters, they wouldn't be so far ahead."

Helen snorted. "It was tried by some smarties from the planet Phrygia."

"And?"

Dorn Horsten took over again. "These Dawnworld inhabitants don't take kindly to being intruded upon. They have no need for trade, no desire for intercourse with otherworldlings. So when somebody comes along and stirs up their . . . anthill, if you will, they take measures."

"Such as what?"

"They evidently have a little trick of tracing the intruders back to the world, or worlds, of their origin and making a slight switch in the atmosphere. Phrygia, which once had a human population of a couple of billion, now has a methane-hydrogen-ammonia atmosphere which proves difficult to breathe. In short, there are no more Phrygians."

Zorro shifted in his chair unhappily. "Still, there should be some way. Evidently, these burros from Phrygia antagonized the, uh, Dawnworlders, or showed their hand in some manner or other."

"Evidently," Helen said, complete with sarcasm, "but I wouldn't want to be the next to try. I wouldn't even want to be a citizen of the planet from which the next who tries hails. And according to Ronny Bronston and Phil Birdman, the two Section G agents who handled the case, it was nip and tuck whether or not the Dawnmen finished off the whole three thousand planets we humans have colonized so far. Happily, for some reason, they seemed to think Phrygia would be enough. But next time?"

"It'd have to be done right," Zorro argued stubbornly.

"It sure as hell would," Helen said. "So forget about it." She shivered. "Just thinking about messing around with those zombies gives me the willies."

Zorro said, "Where are the so-called Dawnworlds located, anyway?"

"They aren't on the starcharts," Horsten told him. "That's certain. The big wigs at the Octagon are scared silly that some scatterbrains will hear about such items as the matter converters and get all steamed up with man's oldest dream."

"Oldest dream?" Jerry said.

"The philosopher's stone. The old alchemy bit. Changing base metals to gold. Evidently, the Dawnmen go them one further, they can change anything to gold, or anything else. I suppose you could put a Rembrandt in one end of it and bring out a perfect twin from the other, or any number of them."

"What's a Rembrandt?" Zorro Juarez scowled.

"An old, old Earth painter. I believe some works still to be found in museums are attributed to him. At any rate, Ross Metaxa and the other powers that be are afraid that with a trillion or so people in our confederation of planets, there'll be some avaricious enough to pull down the roof on all of us, in their greed to sneak a matter converter from under the noses of the Dawnmen."

"Well . . . if they're not intelligent . . ." Zorro muttered.

Helen snarled at him, "Don't be dense, lover. They don't have to be intelligent to push a button or throw a switch. They've got defenses we've never even dreamed of." Her voice took on a childish treble. "I don't want to marry anybody else, Uncle Zorro. I wanta marry you."

Zorro Juarez did a double take.

From the doorway, Helmut Brinker said, "Citizen Rhodes, you wanted to be shown around the hydroponics compartments. I didn't have time, yesterday."

"Oh, sure." Jerry Rhodes came to his feet.

With a skip and a jump, Helen had bounced onto Zorro's lap and threw her arms around his neck. He rolled his eyes up in resignation.

Dorn Horsten said, "Now, Helen, you're pestering Citizen Juarez."

"No I'm not, Daddy. Am I, Uncle Zorro? Uncle Zorro is going to marry me. Everybody has to marry somebody, don't they, Uncle Zorro?" Without waiting for an answer to that, she added definitely, "Uncle Zorro is gonna marry me. He likes girls. Don't you, Uncle Zorro?"

"Stop squirming, you little witch," he growled under his breath. Aloud, he said, "Sometimes."

She said, her eyes wide, "You like boys better than girls, Uncle Zorro? I like boys better than girls, but I thought maybe you liked girls."

Not even his darkish complexion completely hid the red creeping up the unfortunate's neck.

Jerry Rhodes was chuckling as he joined the second officer of the *Half Moon*. He said, "I thought possibly you came back to try another round of battle chess."

The ship's officer didn't answer that but rather turned abruptly and led the way from the ship's lounge.

When the door closed behind them, Helen vaulted down from Zorro's lap and, hands on hips, looked after the two.

Zorro snapped, "Look, fun is fun, but I'm getting tired of this running gag. And just for the record, damn it, sooner or later that double innuendo of yours is going to get through to even somebody as dense as Helmut Brinker, and people are going to start wondering how a knee-high eight-year-old gets off cracks you usually hear in a burlesque revival."

Helen ignored him. "I don't like that."

"You don't like what?" Zorro growled.

23

Dorn looked at her too.

"I don't like that sorehead Brinker going off with Jerry. Jerry's too easy-going. He doesn't know a wrong guy when he sees one."

Jerry Rhodes, hands in pockets, strolled easily after the ship's officer, down the companionway. Keeping in mind his role as playboy and the need for practicing it, he kept going a running patter.

"Fascinatin', you know," he said. "Demmed fascinatin'. Never traveled on a passenger freighter before. Roughing it, eh? If Mother could see me now. Horrified, eh? Associating with characters such as this Zorro Juarez, eh? In trade, mind you. Peddles cattle, or some such. Beef cattle, he says. Always wondered, vaguely, where beef steaks came from. Evidently, they cut them off of animals. Fascinatin'."

The second officer growled something coldly, not turning his head. He was in a fury but Jerry Rhodes chose to ignore it. There was a something in the heavy-set Brinker that egged you on, that made you want to needle him. Jerry Rhodes felt an edge of shame at himself, but there was a boring element in travel on the *Half Moon* and he couldn't keep from provoking the other.

He pattered, "And associating with the crew, mind you. Ha, Mother! You can't imagine, Mother!"

"That's what you think," Helmut Brinker muttered beneath his breath. "Here. Here's the key hydroponics compartment. Nothing much to see, really." He activated a metal door, and stepped forward.

Jerry Rhodes entered, too, and stepped past the other to stare at the level upon level of plants which filled the extensive room from bulkhead to bulkhead and from deck to overhead. "Fascinatin'," he said.

"You know what they eat?" Brinker demanded. And then, without waiting for an answer, "Anything. Garbage, human excreta, wastepaper—anything. You know what'd happen if you fell into one of those tanks?"

"Holy Ultimate!" Jerry Rhodes grunted in amused protest.

Brinker grabbed him roughly by an arm and hauled him about.

"Listen," he growled, "I'm short of credits, understand? I figure you owe me for those two games. I had them won."

Jerry pulled away and took half a dozen steps to the rear. "Now look here!"

"I'm looking at you. Right at you, you fancy molly. And I want those credits!"

Jerry Rhodes was not above indignation, even when confronted by these odds. He took another couple of steps backward, but put up his hands in an ineffectual display of defense.

"Not with these tactics," he got out.

"All right," the other said, rage growing. "You asked for this, smart pockets. That wrist chronometer you're wearing alone . . ." He let the sentence dribble off as he shuffled forward.

Jerry Rhodes' eyes widened.

Behind them, the compartment door swung open and Helen peered in, unseen by the enraged ship's officer. She made a face at Jerry and turned her head, then disappeared.

"Now . . ." Brinker began, his hands reaching.

But Zorro Juarez was at the door, his expression amused. In his hand was his bullwhip. He flicked it, almost lazily. The leather snaked out in a blur, wound about the heel of the second officer's right shoe. There was a quick upward tug, an unbalancing, a cry of utter surprise, a forward collapse, an unhappy crunch of chin hitting metal deck.

Jerry Rhodes looked down at the unconscious sorehead. "Wow," he said in awed wonder. "That sure was luck."

"*Luck!*" Helen snarled at him, as she reappeared in the doorway. "Why, you stupid jerk! If we hadn't followed, this overgrown pig would have clobbered you."

"Um," he told her, in heartfelt earnestness. "That's what I meant. I sure am lucky you two showed up."

III

THEY HAD little to go on, when the *Half Moon* set down on Firenze. In fact, had decided, in conference, that there was surprisingly little known about the workings of the subversive wracked world. After all, it had been a member of United Planets for the better part of a century. During that time, a considerable dossier should have accumulated, based on the reports of Section G and other U.P. personnel assigned there. However, after assimilating what reports Irene Kasansky had given them, immediately before departure, they realized how preciously scant the supposed inside information was.

"These people are really security conscious," Dorn Horsten had mutterd, frowning down at the thin sheaf of study material.

"We'll have to play it by ear," Helen said, as unhappy as her oversized partner.

Jerry said, "Well, it's all rather simple. They're plagued by an underground. Our job is to locate these subversives and do them in. With a little luck . . ."

They bent on him a simultaneous glower.

Jerry swallowed apologetically and shut up.

Zorro said, "We'd better destroy these papers. It wouldn't do to try to land with anything connecting us to Section G."

It turned out that their destination had exactly one spaceport. It was indicative of the restrictions Firenze's situation had imposed. There were, throughout the United Planets Confederation, various worlds that minimized the amount of intercourse with fellow planets. But, invariably, these were the most reactionary, backward members of man's far-flung league, worlds whose ruling classes could not afford to allow their populations to come in contact with peoples who had solved man's immediate socioeconomic problems and had achieved to a high degree of freedom.

There were quite a number of such planets thrown up in the race's chaotic populating of this sector of the galaxy. Usually, worlds based on one type of dictatorship or another, ranging from theocracies to technocracies, in few of which the ruling elite were actually elite—although when the politico-economic system had been originated, perhaps they had been.

Possibly, the least valid method of choosing a ruling class has been the most widely utilized by the human race: nepotism. In primitive society, it must have been unknown, or practically so. When representation was based on the sib, clan, or gens and chiefs were elected on their merit, there was little reason for such a tribal official to wish to hand down his office to his son. There was no profit motive, since the job was not remunerative, a chief being not better off materially than any other member of the tribe. However, as society evolved and the powers of the chiefs —and priests—of necessity expanded, they had little time to hunt their own game, or till their own fields, as Odysseus was found doing when Agamemnon, Menelaus, and Palamedes came to recruit him for the police action against Illium. It became necessary for society as a whole to provide for their elected rulers and in time the jobs became worth having, leisure being the ultimate luxury in a society where abundance is but a dream. And, shortly, such offices became no longer elective, as strongman and holyman subverted primitive institutions.

Be all this as it may, it was distressing for the operatives of Section G to see such indications of the police state as but one port of entry to a whole planet as advanced as Firenze. Among other things, it meant restrictions on commerce and exchange of technological knowledge, and this, above all, was what their department was interested in fostering.

Their small group were the only ones disembarking on Firenze. For that matter, they had been the only passengers aboard the *Half Moon,* which, although licensed to carry travelers, was so haphazardly scheduled that it was seldom practical. While the robos unloaded their luggage, and such freight as had been designated for this set down, the four of them, still pretending to be comparative strangers, took a spaceport ground vehicle to the administration building, the surly second officer accompanying them, to handle any red tape that might evolve.

By the half-puzzled looks he sometimes shot from the corner of his eyes at Jerry Rhodes, it could be seen that Helmut Brinker was still not quite clear on what had happened. In his memory, evidently, one moment he had been heading for the foppish Jerry, to wring from him either the credits Brinker considered he had coming to him, or his pound of flesh, from the other's none too brawny frame. The next moment, black had become the color of the day, and when he had awakened, it was with an egg-sized bump on his chin and utter disbelief in his mind.

Helen, her small, chubby hands folded demurely in her lap, had been gazing at him in the unblinking quizzicalness of pre-adolescence, since they had first mounted the air-cushion cart.

Finally she blurted, "Mr. Second Officer Blinker, you got two chins."

"Helen!" Dorn Horsten said.

She looked at her supposed father. "Well, he has, Daddy. Hasn't he, Uncle Zorro? One of 'em's blue. You got two chins, Mr. Blinker, and one of 'em's blue." She added, from accumulated wisdom, "Most people only got one chin."

Helmut Brinker scowled at her. "Brinker," he said.

"Brinker what?"

"My name's Brinker, not Blinker," he growled in disgust.

"That's what I said," she said with satisfaction. "And two chins."

"Helen," Dorn Horsten said in mild reproof, "Citizen Brinker is the same as everyone else. He has only one chin. Now, that will be all. Please be on your best behavior at the administration building."

Helen looked skeptically at the second officer's lower face. She turned her eyes to Zorro and then Jerry Rhodes, as though seeking corroboration. However, those two worthies looked away. Helen returned to observing the chin—or chins —in question and muttering to herself under her breath.

"That will be all, Helen," her father said, and, evidently to take the conversation out of the hands of his disconcerting daughter, added to Helmut Brinker, "Are none of the crew to take, ah, port-leave here? I would think they would welcome the opportunity."

The second officer snorted. "On this planet? If the skipper let ten men off on an overnight pass, three'd get themselves shot in duels, as easy's they'd get a black eye and a hangover on some good shore-leave world like, say, Shangri-La. And four of the others'd be in the brig for something subversive, like preferring vanilla to chocolate ice cream." He snorted sourly again.

The driver of the spaceport runabout swiveled in his seat and looked at Helmut Brinker. He said evenly, "You an Engelist, or something?"

"Holy Jumpin' Zen, no," the *Half Moon*'s second officer blurted. "I was just kidding."

The driver continued to look at him for a long moment, finally, after darting a glance back at the tarmac to check his course, he said, "Maybe you don't like Firenze? Maybe you think you can toss insults around about the planet of my birth, right in front of me. I'm just a nobody, without enough guts to call you out."

"Holy Ultimate," the second muttered. "If I get myself skewered in some silly duel, the skipper'll crucify me." He looked earnestly at the Florentine. "Look, fella, I'm *sorry*. I apologize. I love this planet, uh, Firenze. I was just joking."

The driver began to turn back to his task of piloting, when Jerry Rhodes began to laugh.

The Florentine's face became a mask. "What's funny Signore?"

But Helen was in there. She shook her finger at the transportation cart's chauffeur. "Now, you stop turning around all the time and talking and all. You scare me. I never rode in one of these things afore, and you turn around all the time and get mad, and you scare me. And

28

I don't like it here. And"—she topped it—"I'll tell my daddy!"

"Now, Helen," her father said.

"I wanna go home!" Helen shrilled.

The driver turned back to his duties and hunched his shoulders.

Zorro Juarez cleared his throat and said to the Florentine, as though seeking a subject with which to clear the air, "What is an Engelist?"

It was evidently the wrong subject to have chosen.

The other said, "You don't know what an Engelist is? What kind of world you come from?" And then in confused contradiction of himself, "You live on some sort of Engelist government world?"

Zorro said, in unwonted mildness, "I'm from Vacamundo. We don't have any Engelists, or whatever you call them, there. What's an Engelist?"

They were almost to the entry of the official building. However, the driver took Zorro in with a slow calculation. "How do I know you're not some undercover police, trying to egg me into indicating I got unusual interest in the Engelists?"

Zorro shook his head at him in true puzzlement. "Come again on that?"

The driver turned his back abruptly, and did things with his cart controls.

They pulled up before the short flight of stairs which mounted to the building's portals, and the driver dropped the lift lever and disembarked to open doors for them. His face was darkly suspicious and he spoke no further. Helen, when her father wasn't looking, stuck her tongue out at him before tripping after the rest.

At the top of the stone stairway were three guards, two of them bearing muffle rifles. They came to the salute, eyes straight ahead. A trim sub-officer, a quick-draw holster at his hip, came forward, his face expressionless.

The second officer of the *Half Moon* had evidently been through Firenze routine before. He stepped out and presented a clipboard of papers.

"Four passengers from the *Half Moon*. Origin, Earth. Visas for Firenze entry in order."

The sub-officer looked at Brinker carefully. He took the clipboard. Before looking at it, he weighed the four in question, one by one, with care. Finally, he looked down at the papers. He took his time perusing them.

He said at last, "Very well, follow me." He turned and

led the way to the entry. The party from the *Half Moon* trailed behind.

Zorro growled under his breath, "Some welcome for a bunch of newcomers."

Dorn Horsten said, an edge of irritation in his voice, "See here, I expected someone from the University. . . ."

The Florentine said, "After clearance."

The big scientist pushed his pince-nez glasses back onto his nose. "Stuff and nonsense," he muttered.

The sub-officer paused. "Are you criticizing the institutions of the Free Democracy of the Commonwealth of Firenze, or me, personally?"

But Helen was in there again. She pointed a finger at the Firenze official, her other small fist on her hip. "You leave my daddy alone," she said in warning.

The sub-officer looked at her. He frowned puzzlement. He looked back at her father. Dorn Horsten stood there scowling, but evidently unrepentant.

The Florentine started over again. "I will brook no criticism of the institutions. . . ."

Helen took a half skip forward and let him have it on the shins. "I *told* you to leave my daddy alone, you nasty thing. My daddy didn't bother you."

"Helen!" Horsten blurted.

Zorro Juarez scooped her up and held her under his left arm. He tapped his tranca against his trouser leg. "Let's get on with it," he said.

"Lemme go!" Helen shrilled.

The Florentine sub-officer stood there, either counting to himself or communicating with whatever gods he followed. He had closed his eyes in mental, rather than physical, anguish.

Finally, he opened them and said emotionlessly, "Follow me."

Zorro kept his grip on the kicking Helen.

"I don't *like* this place. I wanna go *home*," she howled.

The sub-officer held the door open for them. Zorro, laden down with Helen, passed through last. The sub-officer closed his eyes again, when she went by. It was just as well; she was sticking her tongue out in impotent rage.

Immediately inside the door was a large desk, behind it an older and more elaborately uniformed Florentine. He took them all in, including the sub-officer, without speaking. When the sub-officer put the clipboard of entry papers before him, he scanned it very slowly. The four passengers from space lined up before the desk, the second officer of the *Half Moon* slightly ahead of them.

The offical looked up finally and stared at Jerry Rhodes, who was at the far right of the lineup. Jerry, hands nonchalantly in his pockets, was looking about the large entry hall.

The Florentine rapped, "Are you, or have you ever been, an Engelist?"

Jerry Rhodes brought his eyes to him, in unfeigned lack of comprehension.

"Me? What's an Engelist? Listen, how do I go about finding a deluxe hotel? The very best. Some place with decent food and some action." He winked at the other, dropped his voice slightly and spoke from the side of his mouth. "You know, nice nightspot, vintage guzzle, pick up a good looking . . ."

The sub-officer clipped, "Answer the Tenente's question!"

Jerry blinked. "Me? No. I don't even know what a . . . whatever you said . . . is."

The tenente went on down the line. And got the same response from Dorn Horsten and Zorro Juarez. That is, a denial that they were or had ever been, Engelists.

The tenente brought out papers and got their signatures to that effect. The papers were added to the clipboard. He handed the clipboard to the sub-officer, who saluted. The tenente returned the salute. He had one last word to say to the newcomers to Firenze.

"In landing upon this planet you foreswear recourse to your own world, or to the United Planets, insofar as political activities are concerned. That is, if it is found that you participate in Firenze internal affairs, such as Engelist subversion, you are subject to our laws and to the government of the First Signore. Is that understood and accepted? If not, you must return to the"—he looked down at the paper before him—"the *Half Moon*, and depart Firenze."

Zorro Juarez said, "You mean, if we get in trouble, we can't appeal to the United Planets Embassy?"

The tenente said, "Why should you get in trouble? You have declared you are not an Engelist, haven't you?"

Jerry Rhodes said, "Is that the only kind of trouble you can get into on this world?"

"Are you attempting to be amusing, Signore, uh . . . Rhodes?"

Jerry said plaintively, "So far, I haven't found anything to be amusing about on this planet. All I want to know is where I can find some decent food and a little action.

31

After a week of Tuesdays on that so-called passenger freighter, what I need is . . ."

Helen, who at long last had been set back on her own feet again, whined, "I don't like this place, Daddy. I wanna go home."

"Now, Helen, be a good girl."

The sub-officer had closed his eyes again, when Helen opened her trap. The tenente said, "That will be all. Take them to customs."

At this point Helmut Brinker called it quits. His duties, evidently, took him no further. He shook hands, even with Jerry Rhodes, patted Helen carefully on the head, as though half suspicious that she might bite him, and set off for the spaceport cart.

Helen held on to Zorro's hand on the way to the next stop. He growled at her from the side of his mouth, "Aren't you overdoing this?"

She looked up at him balefully and snarled in a low voice, "The way I look at it, so far I've stopped two duels. And if you three overgrown clods don't keep your traps shut, I doubt if we'll ever get to the hotel without one of you getting ventilated, or whatever they do in the way of dueling here."

He snorted, but let it go.

The natty sub-officer pushed through another door and led the way to customs inspection where the robos had obviously piled their luggage. On their appearance, three inspectors, under what was obviously a customs official, began opening bags and trunks.

"Hey," Jerry said in mild protest at their indifferent handling of his luxurious trappings.

The sub-officer handed the clipboard to the customs man, who looked at Jerry Rhodes in speculation. "You have something to hide?"

"Who me?"

"Do you swear that you have no Engelist propaganda either in your luggage or on your person?"

"Propaganda?" Jerry said blankly.

Dorn Horsten said to him, "An old Amer-English word derived from 'to propagate.' It merely meant the particular doctrines or principles promulgated by an organization, with no suggestion of whether or not the teachings were correct or false. Later, however, the word gained an unsavory connotation and grew synonymous with political lies."

The customs official looked coldly at the scientist. "All

Engelist propaganda is composed of lies. Are you suggesting otherwise?"

"But I've never even read or heard any," Horsten protested.

"You haven't answered my question!" the other snapped. "Do you deny all Engelist propaganda is composed of subversive lies?"

"Well, now . . ."

Helen began to cry. "I gotta go to the *baaathroom.*"

Dorn Horsten looked at the customs inspector plaintively.

The sub-officer sighed in resignation and said, "This way, Dr. Horsten."

Horsten took Helen's hand and they followed the Florentine to a side door and out. The inspector looked after them for a moment, then turned back to his duties.

He had gotten to a rather outsized hatbox a few minutes later and had begun to activate its opening mechanism, when a voice squealed from behind him, "Don't you bother my dolly!" He winced and his shoulders hunched up under the attack of the eight-year-old.

Helen stomped up indignantly and snatched the hatbox from the other's hands.

The chief inspector looked at the harassed Horsten.

Dr. Horsten said, "She's tired."

The inspector said, "All baggage must be thoroughly examined."

Helen had turned her back defiantly and sat down on the floor, the hatbox between her chubby legs.

Zorro said, "I'll help."

He hunkered down on his heels before her and said, "Let's see your dolly."

The inspector and the sub-officer who had been accompanying the travelers since first they had entered the administration building, stood looking down in frustration.

Helen looked suspiciously at Zorro Juarez, as though wondering if she was being betrayed to the enemy by this former ally. However, she touched the box's stud and the top slid open.

"This is Gertrude," she said. And then, proudly, "Gertrude's a boy."

The sub-officer muttered something and the inspector looked at him. "What?"

"Nothing. I'm getting back to my post before . . ."

"Before what?" the chief inspector said accusingly.

"Nothing." The sub-officer left as though in a hurry.

Helen was saying, "And this is his potty."

Zorro, still squated on his heels, began to say, "How does it work?" But then, quickly, "Never mind. What is this?" He reached the potty up in the direction of the inspector for examination, but that official winced and put his hands slightly behind his back.

A quiet technician on the far side of the room, stationed behind a battery of switches and dials, said, "I get an electronic buzz."

The three customs men, who had been bent over the various bags, straightened and looked at him. The inspection chief spun, his eyebrows high.

"Get a level on it!"

Helen was saying, "And this is the washin' machine. You wanna see me wash his jerkin?"

"No," Zorro said.

"You put it in here," she said.

The technician, registering disbelief, had come to his feet and approached Helen. Zorro stood up.

The technician pointed at the hatbox. "It comes from there."

The inspector's eyes narrowed and he looked at Horsten.

"Oh, good heavens," Dr. Horsten said. He pushed his pince-nez glasses back, as though preparatory to a lengthy discussion.

The technician stooped and came up with a gadget that neatly fit into his hand. He stared at it.

"Hey," Helen said in indignation. "That's my Gertrude's stove."

The technician flicked a stud with the nail of his little finger, then shifted his grip on the toy hurriedly as he obviously burned himself. He looked at the inspector in awe. "See that little thing, there?" He indicated. "That must be the smallest powerpack I've ever seen."

The inspector glared at him. "Put it back," he said.

"Yes, sir." The technician put it back and returned to his post.

Dr. Horsten said to Helen, "Put your toys away, dear. You can play when we get to the hotel."

"I don't wanna go to the hotel. I wanna go home. I hate this place. This place is . . ." She thought about it, then finished definitely, ". . . a dump."

The inspector gave up on this front. He turned on Zorro. "What's that you have in your hand, a weapon? Let me see it."

34

"Weapon?" Zorro said. "This is my tranca." He held up the leather swagger stick.

"What is a tranca?" the inspector said in suspicion.

"Why . . ." Zorro looked down at it, as though that was the last question he had ever expected to hear. "How could one tell a gentleman gaucho from a vaquero unless he carried a tranca?"

The inspector looked at him sarcastically and took the leather object in question. He stared down at it, hefted it. Finally, he took it over to the technician and held it before a screen.

"Take a reading on this."

"It reads clean. Some very hard leather, maybe some rubber. Not enough metal to make any difference."

The inspector took it back to Zorro, puzzled. "What do you do with it?"

Zorro returned the puzzlement. "Do with it? I *carry* it. I'm a gaucho." His voice went stiff. "Do you doubt my word that I am a gaucho?"

The inspector straightened and his face went expressionless. "It was not my desire to question your veracity, Signore. However, if honor is involved . . ."

Two of his men stepped forward and stood at his side at attention. One of them said, "If the Inspector requires seconds . . ."

Dr. Horsten said hurriedly, "Gentlemen, gentlemen. You are of different worlds and do not understand each other's institutions. Certainly, you are both men of honor. All a misunderstanding . . ."

Jerry Rhodes suddenly broke into laughter.

All eyes went to him. All coldly, save those of Dr. Horsten, who expressed anguish.

The inspector said, "Yes, Signore, uh, Rhodes?"

Helen said shrilly, "Uncle Jerry, you stop laughing at the way I change Gertrude's diddies."

Jerry was looking at the other men, his eyes slightly wide. He looked down at Helen quickly. "I'm sorry, honey," he said. "You change them very nicely."

The inspector turned back to Zorro Juarez. "I am at your service, if you feel need of satisfaction. Undoubtedly, these gentlemen, your fellow travelers, will act for you."

"Now . . ." Dorn Horsten began hurriedly.

There was a small clatter.

All eyes went to the floor.

There was a badge laying there.

It was a simple bronze badge, and the standing men

could read of its inscription only, SECTION G, and less clearly, part of the smaller lettering, *Interplanetary Department of Justice*.

The chief inspector was bug-eyed.

"What's *that?*" he snapped.

Helen reached. "You can't have my Junior Section G badge," she howled, grabbing for it.

But one of the customs men was staring at Jerry Rhodes. "That badge dropped from . . ." he began.

From the open doorway, through which they had entered the room, Dorn Horsten roared, "*Earthquake!* Everybody get under something! Helen, quick!"

Zorro Juarez was not slow on the uptake. He waved his arms frantically. "Under the doorway, or a desk. If the roof falls in, you're safer!"

Dr. Horsten was swaying desperately, his arms holding onto the doorjamb, one on each side. "Earthquake!" he roared again. "Helen!"

The room was shaking. A picture on the wall of a stern faced, uniformed personage of obviously high rank was swaying pendulum-like back and forth.

The faces of the Florentines registered shock. They froze momentarily.

"Under something!" Zorro yelled. "If the roof gives way . . ."

Helen had darted a look of comprehension at her supposed father, then, screaming, flew to the customs officer who had, a moment earlier, begun to accuse Jerry Rhodes of something. She jumped up against him, throwing her chubby legs around his waist, holding onto him for dear life. "Save me! Save me!" And even as she screamed at that confused worthy, one of her deft tiny hands was extracting what seemed a safety pin from her little girl playsuit.

IV

MOMENTS LATER, Dr. Horsten, the celebrated algae specialist, let go of the doorjamb onto which he had been hanging for dear life, and took a white handkerchief from a jerkin pocket to wipe his forehead. He then took the pince-nez glasses from his nose and wiped them.

He sighed relief. "I'm terrified of earthquakes," he announced.

The balance of the room's occupants were disposed here

36

and there. Zorro and the chief customs inspector were cowering under the doorway through which Helen and her father had departed for the ladies' room earlier, and to which Zorro had dragged the other. Jerry was under the inspector's desk, evidently on the verge of hysteria, since he was laughing madly. The other two customs men were below the long table upon which sat the baggage, Helen beside them and childishly giggling at the fun.

They began to crawl, or stagger, to the room's center again.

"I once lived in Japan," Horsten explained to all. "Only thing to do in an earthquake. Get below the overhead of a door. When the roof caves in, you're comparatively safe."

"That's the way we do it on Vacamundo," Zorro Juarez confirmed.

The inspector, his face slightly dazed, said, "Thank you, thank you, Signore. I've . . . I've never been in an earthquake before. It's the first one I've ever even heard of on Firenze." He shook his head. "What's the matter with Rudolf?"

Rudolf was the examiner who had been chosen by Helen to save her, in the excitement of the quake. There was a glazed something in his face.

Dorn Horsten stepped nearer and looked into the man's eyes. He reached out and pulled down one of the other's eyelids.

"Shock," he announced.

The inspector looked at him. "Are you an M.D.? I thought your doctorate . . ."

Dorn Horsten puffed out his cheeks. "I have eight doctorates, my good man. My M.D. was taken in Vienna when I was but a lad. This man should be put to bed at once and covered warmly. Give him a double shot of, uh, the best of guzzle, whatever it is alcoholic you drink on this planet. He'll be all right tomorrow."

A new voice from the doorway that Horsten had just abandoned said, "What in the name of the Holy Ultimate is going on?"

The inspector turned, came to rigid attention, as did his men—save for Rudolf.

"Yes, Your Eccellenza. The earthquake. Was the damage bad?"

The newcomer was a man in his early middle years. He was physically fit, keen of expression and wore his clothes as though he had never known a suit out of press, a shirt with the slightest wilt, in all his days.

He looked about the room, then at each of its occupants, in turn. He eventually got back to the chief inspector. "What are you talking about, Grossi?"

Inspector Grossi said, "The earthquake, Eccellenza."

"Are you mad?" But then his expression altered infinitesimally. "You know, I did feel, as I approached this room, a slight shaking."

Horsten said, mopping his brow again, "That's the way it is. Some people go right through a quake and don't even recognize it."

The newcomer considered him, then turned and stared at the wooden faced Rudolf. "What's wrong with him?"

Zorro Juarez spoke up smoothly. "He was terrified. I was watching him. He must have some sort of phobia about earthquakes. He froze with fear."

"That seems hard to believe. Earthquakes are all but unknown on Firenze. The only acquaintance I, myself, have had with them is through reading."

Zorro shrugged. "Scared to death," he said. He shook his head. "You Florentines seem to frighten easily."

A chill went through the room.

The inspector and one of his men spoke simultaneously. "I demand satisfaction!"

But the newcomer held up a hand. "Please, Signori. These visitors from overspace are our honored guests. Besides, you are all obviously upset. See that this man"—he stared again, unbelievingly, at Rudolf—"is taken care of."

He turned to the travelers, and to Dorn Horsten in particular. "Undoubtedly, Signore, you are the celebrated Dr. Horsten. May I introduce myself?" He clicked his heels, bowed ever so slightly from the waist. "Maggiore Roberto Verona, of the staff of His Eccellenza, the Third Signore."

Dr. Horsten was not to be outdone in the amenities, his own bow was even slighter than the other, albeit, if anything, more formal. "Pleasure, Maggiore. And may I present my daughter, Helen. . . ."

Helen, her eyes bright, took the hem of her very short skirt in her hands and dropped a perfect curtsy, ignoring the sigh that indicated relief from her father.

The maggiore, obviously to the manor born, bowed again more deeply. "Signorina." He smiled. "I am ravished."

Customs Inspector Grossi cleared his throat at that.

Dorn Horsten was saying, "And these gentlemen are fellow passengers from the *Half Moon*. Citizens, uh, Zorro Juarez, from the planet, uh . . ."

"Vacamundo," Zorro supplied.

"Yes, of course. And, uh, Gerald Rhodes from, uh, now don't tell me," Horsten dithered.

Jerry said, "If you're from the tourist bureau, or whatever, what I want is some hotel, the best, of course, where . . ."

Chief Inspector Grossi, in horror, said, "Signore Rhodes! His Eccellenza . . ."

But Roberto Verona was amused. "Citizen Rhodes, we shall do what we can. Am I to understand you have made no reservations for your stay on Firenze?"

"I never bother with reservations," Jerry told him. "I always figure, let the other man make the reservations, then I cross the clerk's palm with a bit of hard credit and—like magic—I've got the best suite in the house."

The maggiore made an amused moue. "My dear Signore Rhodes, believe me, I have been overspace on a few occasions myself and hence am somewhat familiar with usage on other worlds. However, forgive me, I would not suggest you offer the *mancia* to a male citizen of Firenze. He would most certainly call you out."

"*Mancia?* Call me out?" Jerry said blankly.

Zorro growled, "Evidently, try to tip a man here and he wants to duel you."

The newcomer looked at Dr. Horsten. "You, of course, have reservations at the *Albergo Palazzo*. If I may say so, Doctor, Academician Udine is most excited at your arrival. It is not every day that a scientist of your attainments honors Firenze."

"You are too kind."

Zorro said, "The *Palazzo*. That's the hotel I sent a subspace cable to for a room."

The maggiore said politely, "Most interplanetary visitors at least begin their sojourn on Firenze at the *Palazzo*, 'Signore Juarez."

Jerry said, "Well, I might as well check in there too. I hope they've got accommodations suitable to my standing."

The other was frowning. "Unfortunately, Signore, there is a shortage. You see, His *Zelenza* and his Cabinet are due for a convention preceding the pseudo-election here in Firenze, beginning tomorrow." He looked back at Dr. Horsten. "One of the reasons I met you was because the Third Signore suggested I see that you find some sort of quarters, no matter what."

"The Third Signore?" Dorn Horsten frowned.

"There are nine Signori in the Cabinet of the First

Signore, our executive head," the maggiore explained smoothly.

"Ah, I see. And what portfolio does the Third Signore carry?"

"Anti-Subversion," the maggiore said pleasantly.

Helen said, "I'm tired. I want my nap. Gertrude wants his nap. I'm *awful* tired." She added, to clinch it, "I hate this dump."

The maggiore looked at Inspector Grossi, who said, "The baggage of the outworlders has been inspected, Eccellenza."

"Very well, Inspector." Roberto Verona made a sweeping gesture with his right hand. "This way, Signorina, Signori. . . ."

Helen took his hand and looked up at him. "Gee, you do that pretty."

He smiled winningly down at her. "Do what, little Signorina?" They passed through the door into the corridor beyond.

"Make that sissy motion with your hand," she said flatly.

His smile faded.

He said to Dr. Horsten, as the others fell in behind, "You know, an earthquake is quite unique here."

"This must have been the very center." Horsten nodded. "It doesn't seem to have affected the vicinity."

"Ah, you need not have worried. This building is well constructed. It would have been really difficult for even an earthquake to shake it."

"You're telling me," Horsten muttered.

"I beg your pardon?"

"I said, it seems to be," the scientist told him in agreement.

Outside the administration building a suitably impressive hover-limousine was pulled up at the curb.

Even as he bowed them into the chauffeur driven vehicle the maggiore was saying, "I am sure that there will be ample room for all, since our destination is the same."

"You're sure you're not from the tourist . . ." Jerry began again, even as he ducked his head to take the front seat next to the driver.

The maggiore had visibly flinched, and his smile had sagged, but Zorro covered.

"The major is a high government official, Jerry. He's come to welcome the doctor. All we're doing is hitching a ride."

"Ha!" Jerry said. "Fascinating. If Mother could only hear that. Surprised the old girl didn't send ahead. Some sort of boring reception committee. Interplanetary WCTU or SPCA, or DRR, or something. Mother belongs to everything." He added absently, "Everything she doesn't own."

Dorn Horsten, if only to keep the conversation going, said, "I've heard of the Interplanetary WCTU and of the SPCA, but the DRR eludes me."

"Daughters of the Russian Revolution," Jerry said. "One of my great-great grandmothers was from Leningrad. Very conservative outfit. Bunch of old hens. Flag wavers. You know the type. Origins of the outfit lost way back in the mists of antiquity."

"Revolution?" Maggiore Verona said, his voice slightly less suave. "Upon Firenze, we frown upon that term, Signore."

Horsten said, in quick cover, "If my studies of boyhood serve me, Citizen Rhodes refers to a revolution that took place a long time ago, Maggiore. I have found that revolutions become acceptable in proportion to the time that has elapsed since their inception. Lucius Brutus and Collatinus were on the wild-eyed fanatic side when they overthrew the Tarquins, however, as the centuries passed, these founders of the Republic gained acceptability, and later comers, such as the first Caesars, were happy to be able to trace themselves back to the Julian and Claudian gentes which were instrumental in expelling the Etruscans. Later, in history, the better elements in the British American colonies fled to Canada or back to the motherland before the fury of the mob, which, fanned to a white heat by Sam Adams and Tom Paine, and led by malcontents such as Washington, dubbed themselves Sons of Liberty and stole, burned and destroyed the property of the Tories. But in a century or so the posterity of those mobs became the most conservative members of a now conservative nation and proudly claimed the descent."

Jerry Rhodes yawned. Helen was rocking her doll in her arms and crooning something about three little girls in blue, tra la.

"Sons of Liberty?" the maggiore said. "It has been my experience that organizations with such titles are inclined to be subversive." He hastened to add: "Of course, Firenze follows the democratic ethic, however, there is a limit to liberty. For instance, you wouldn't allow someone to stand up in a crowded theater and shout *Fire!* in the name of freedom of speech."

"Why not?" Jerry said innocently. "Certainly, freedom of speech is more important than a few theaters full of

41

people. Besides, somebody else has the right to stand up and yell, *He's a liar, there is no fire!"*

Zorro shook his head at him unobtrusively.

The maggiore looked at Jerry in growing suspicion.

But Jerry Rhodes was happily underway.

"It reminds me of a historical period on Mother Earth I had studied when I was attending the university. All the major nations of the time were continually sounding off about liberty and freedom and democracy. They'd send off expeditionary forces of hundreds of thousands of men, all equipped with the latest military devices, to preserve the liberties of some people halfway around the world from them; people who often didn't have the vaguest idea of what the word meant. Then a Negro—or a Jew or Hindu —would get up in the square of his town and try to sound off about local injustices. Sixteen cops would jump him and run him in, on the grounds that by his exercising these liberties he supposedly had, he was threatening to upset the peace. He might irritate some uneducated slobs, by saying something they didn't like to hear."

Jerry chuckled amusement. "It was a great situation. The powers that be were willing to kill off hundreds of thousands of gooks, abroad, to preserve their liberties such as freedom of speech, but they allowed that liberty in their own country just so long as people said what they liked to hear. You could write anything you wanted, but so far as getting into print in the mass media was concerned, it had a dim chance if you weren't writing what they wanted to read. You could vote for anybody you wanted to, just so long as it was one of their candidates—election laws made it practically impossible for anybody else to get on the ballot. You could demonstrate in the streets until . . ."

Dr. Horsten put in hurriedly, his voice rising above his young colleague's, "Ah, Maggiore Verona, although this is not my first visit to your estimable world, I must confess a considerable ignorance of your institutions. I note that you use a certain amount of terminology foreign to Earth Basic."

The Florentine had been staring at Jerry, but now he shook his head slightly and turned to the scientist. "You are probably referring, my dear Doctor, to an admitted bit of affectation. The first colonizing ships to land on Firenze, though immediately from the planet Avalon, originally came from the most elite section of Mother Earth —Italy."

"Wops," Helen muttered, rocking the doll vigorously.

The maggiore did a double take. *"What?"* he said, his voice unbelieving.

Helen tossed Gertrude up high. "Whoops!" she said. "Whoops we go."

The maggiore, his expression slightly shaken, looked back at the bland faced scientist. "At any rate, a few words of the mother tongue are still retained."

"I see." Horsten nodded.

The chauffeur said something over his shoulder and the maggiore announced, "Here we are, the *Albergo Palazzo*." He opened his own door before the driver could get around to it, and helped the others from their places. Half a dozen hotel employees darted forward to assist.

On the way to the reception desk, the self-named assistant to the Third Signore was in apology.

"You have no idea, Signore Horsten, how short hotel accommodations are. Firenze—the capital city, you know, has the same name as the planet—is packed. But packed, Doctor. We are desolated, but we have had to reserve for you and Signorina Helen what was formerly a single room, on the ground floor, behind the main dining hall."

"Oh, I'm sure we'll manage," the doctor murmured, somewhat taken aback.

"And you, Signore," Roberto Verona said to Zorro. "This is most regrettable. The room of an assistant janitor, down in the basement, has been requisitioned as an emergency measure."

Zorro Juarez winced. "Oh, great," he growled.

Jerry said, "How about me?"

The Florentine rubbed his hand over his mouth. He said, finally, "We'll . . . we'll have to see, Signore Rhodes."

Helen looked up at Jerry from the side of her eyes, and snorted amusement. She had her doll under one arm, her hatbox of toys held in her other hand.

At the reception desk, the Horstens and Zorro were taken care of quickly and with the ambiance of another era. The Section G operatives had already noticed, in mild surprise, the presence of bellhops. Evidently the carry-over of Latin temperament had led to various anachronisms so far as hotels were concerned on Firenze.

But then the morning-suited dignitary officiating as reservation clerk looked at Jerry Rhodes. "Yes, sir?" he said.

Maggiore Verona spoke up, an element of despair in his voice. "Ah, the Signore Rhodes is an honored guest from the planet Catalina. If it is at all possible . . ." He let his sentence sink away, knowing full well the *Palazzo* was packed to the rafters.

But the clerk broke into a beam. He evidently had misinterpreted the government official's concern about Jerry. He gushed, "But how fortunate, sir!"

Jerry said, his voice off-hand, "I'd like the largest suite you have available. Something in tune with my standing."

Helen snickered.

The reception clerk gushed, "By the most fortunate of circumstances, Signore, we have just received a message from the First Signore's secretary, informing us he will not attend the convention. Hence, his suite will be available."

"Gurg," the maggiore said.

"That should do it." Jerry nodded.

"Oh no," Helen muttered.

Jerry turned to Dr. Horsten, grinning hospitably. "I say, Doc. It occurs to me . . ." He turned back to the clerk. "How many rooms in this suite? Bedrooms?"

"Why, Signore, there are six, not including the master bedroom of the First Signore, when he is in residence. Six and six baths, and . . ."

Jerry turned again and spread his hands. "Fine. Doc, you and little Helen. Move in with me. You won't bother me at all." He hesitated slightly, but then turned on his hospitality once again. "You too, Juarez. That janitor's room of yours wouldn't be any too comfortable."

Zorro hesitated, his dark face unhappy. "Well . . . thanks," he said. "A janitor's room isn't exactly the place I'd like to take business contacts."

Jerry waved a hand nonchalantly. "Then it's all settled." He turned to the maggiore. "See that they send up all the bags, eh, like a good chap."

The assistant of the Third Signore flinched.

On the way up to the penthouse, where the suite of the First Signore was located, Helen kept her eyes on Jerry accusingly. She said, a nasty element in her voice, "I'm not even going to ask how you ever pulled that off. I know the answer."

Jerry grinned condescendingly at her.

Helen snorted disgust.

The maggiore had bid them temporary *addio*, promising to look in to ascertain their needs, after they had become established. So it was that an assistant manager with a host of subservient bellhops saw them to their quarters.

Jerry said airily to that worthy, "See that these lads

are suitably recompensed and the item added to my bill. Be generous, of course. I'm notorious for overtipping."

The hotel official bowed gently, his face expressionless. "I have been informed of otherworld usage, Signore, however, on Firenze, the gratuity is not accepted."

"You can't be serious!"

The other flushed. "But I am, Signore."

"You mean these . . . *boys* . . . aren't interested in, say, an interplanetary credit, split up between them?"

"That is what I mean."

Jerry scoffed overbearingly. "Oh, you're crazy."

One of the bellhops stepped up to the assistant manager. "If the Signore *Direttore* requires a second . . ."

Another of the bellhops stepped up.

Dorn Horsten hurriedly lumbered forward and took the hotel junior official by an arm. He beamed in all friendliness. "Ah, thank you ever so much. Wonderful hotel, you have here, Signore. Wonderful hospitality." He was propelling the other toward the door. "How well staffed! How immaculately clean!"

Zorro held the door open.

When the Florentine and his bevy of bellhops were gone, Zorro leaned back against the door and ran a hand over his forehead. "Whew," he whewed. Then he allowed himself a glare at Jerry.

Jerry said, "When I'm told to play a playboy, I play a playboy."

Horsten and Helen were both making faces at him. Helen held a tiny finger to her lips, then showed her teeth at him.

Jerry Rhodes blinked.

Helen tossed her hatbox to a chair, turned Gertrude bottoms-up pulled up the doll's skirt, and twisted something on the toy's back. Helen then handed the doll to her large partner.

Horsten, in turn, took it about the room, holding it toward the light fixtures, the decorations, the furniture, here, there, everywhere, and when one room was done, the next.

The other three followed him, the why-of-it-all becoming obvious even to Jerry Rhodes.

At long last, the scientist halted, his face puzzled. "No signs of the place being bugged whatsoever," he rumbled.

Helen, frowning, deactivated the doll, then snapped her fingers. "You know what?"

They all looked at her.

"It's the suite used by the First Signore, when he's in town. Don't you see? The last place on Firenze that would be bugged." She snorted. "What luck." Then she glared at Jerry. "I take that word back."

Jerry chortled. "Why?" he said. "Here we all are, in the most comfortable quarters in the city. All together, which makes our work that much the easier. And with the perfect excuse for being all together. Where's the bar? There must be a bar in a layout like this. I wonder what kind of guzzle they have on Firenze."

"I noticed one in the main living room," Zorro said. He led the way.

No one was opposed to settling down in a comfort chair or couch. Jerry played host, taking their orders and making up their drinks. As was to be expected, the bar, though not large, was supplied with the most exquisite potables to be found on all the most hedonistically inclined worlds of United Planets.

"This is the life!" Jerry announced, his glass up in a gesture of toast.

Horsten was looking at Helen who had chosen a chair so large that her chubby little legs failed to reach the edge of the seat. She was sitting there with a monstrously big champagne glass and gulping it with considerable satisfaction.

The outsized scientist shook his head. "I'll never get used to it," he said.

Helen finished off about half her drink and then turned to Jerry, her eyes fishy. "Well," she snarled. "What was the stupid idea of dropping that Section G badge right in front of those damned customs men? You trying to get us all shot?"

Jerry was taken aback. His mouth took on an expression that was just short of a pout. "I didn't do it on purpose," he said plaintively.

"I thought we'd agreed to leave everything that might possibly connect us with the Department of Interplanetary Justice back at the Octagon. Suppose they'd searched us."

Jerry looked like an adolescent who'd just been scolded. "Aw," he said. "I'm pretty proud of being a Section G agent. I wanted to carry my badge."

Helen rolled her eyes upward.

Jerry said brightly, "Wasn't it just my luck that earthquake came along? And the customs man, Rudolf, forgetting that the badge dropped out of my jerkin?"

"Earthquake!" Horsten muttered. "I damn near broke my back, shaking that room."

"Forgot!" Helen snarled. "You think it was a cinch, my scratching that Florentine with a memory-wash hypo? He's had three hours cleaned out of his memory. Just keep your fingers crossed some suspicious medico doesn't give him a thorough checking out. That Maggiore Verona can't be as foolish as he looks. If he knew somebody'd gone to the trouble of memory-washing friend Rudolf, he'd want to know why. And they'd go through our luggage like mineral oil."

Horsten winced at her language.

Zorro worked away at his drink and said thoughtfully, "I wonder what would happen if we just came right out and let this Roberto Verona know why we were really here. After all, we're on his side. We're present to help get rid of these Engelists that are evidently bedeviling the planet to the point where nothing can be accomplished."

Dorn Horsten said, "How do you know he's not an Engelist himself?"

Zorro looked at him.

The doctor said impatiently, "Holy Ultimate, man, it's not unpredecented, you know. Evidently, Firenze's underground has infiltrated everywhere. Who is to say they aren't even represented among the First Signore's cabinet, the Second Signore, right on down to the Tenth? For all we know, any or all of them might be Engelists, not to speak of their staffs, such as this Maggiore Verona."

Helen said, "It's no mistake that former Section G operatives have pulled a zero here. This underground is efficient. And you know at what point an underground really gets efficient?"

"When?" Jerry said.

"Just before it takes over," Helen said. "This assignment of ours is going to be accomplished but fast, or we'll wind up with chaos on this planet."

Horsten said unhappily, "Just about anything can happen when a revolution breaks out. The whole planet could be devastated, set back a century or more, so far as progress is concerned."

Zorro finished his drink and chuckled. "I just thought of a wonderful idea for Section G to wrangle its way on just about every planet in the U.P. confederation." He got up from his chair and went to the bar for a refill.

They looked after him, waiting.

He gestured with his glass. "We latch onto one of those

47

matter converters the Dawnworlders have. And we take it to any planet where they still utilize money. Suppose platinum is the means of exchange. Fine, we take one ingot along and duplicate it, over and over again. With it, we bribe every official on the planet, from king, president, holy theocrat, or whatever, down to dog catcher, into the form of socioeconomic system we want."

The other three laughed dutifully.

"Sounds great," Jerry said.

Zorro said, "Just where are these Dawnworlds located, anyway? I was kidding, but you know, it's an idea. If Section G had one of those things at its disposal, what a secret weapon it would be."

"Forget about it," Helen muttered. "In that direction is disaster—for the whole race."

Horsten said, "Where the Dawnworlds are is a top secret, even in Section G. Somewhere beyond the planet Phrygia, of course, but that's almost meaningless, so far as directions are concerned. Phrygia is—or was—the farthest in toward the center of the galaxy that man has thus far settled. But with no more navigating direction than that, you could seek the Dawnworlds forever."

Zorro grunted, only half interested. "Well, somebody must know where they are. After all, a spaceforces ship or so has been out there. What was his name, who handled it?"

"Ronny Bronston," Helen supplied. "Bronston and Agent Birdman."

"Where's Birdman and Bronston now?"

"Birdman's dead, and Ronny's in the hospital," Helen said sourly. "I understand he used to be an easy-going, nice boy type. Now he's Sid Jake's favorite triggerman, one of the best. Don't let that exterior of Sid Jakes fool you. You have to watch these dedicated people. They'll wind up getting you clobbered. There was a guy named Joshua who came from an obscure town called Nazareth. Very dedicated. He had eleven particularly keen followers, but history doesn't record that any of them did so well."

"Very funny," the dark complected agent said.

Horsten finished his drink and set his glass down on a cocktail table. "So much for jabber," he said. "Let's get down to our program of action. What's first on the agenda?"

"We've got to locate this subversive underground," Jerry said. "And with my luck . . ."

"Bounce it." Helen sneered.

The door hummed and they looked up, frowning.

Zorro said, "I wouldn't think Verona would be bothering us this soon."

Horsten lumbered to his feet and walked in the direction of the entry. Helen skipped along beside him, holding a hand. It made a charming scene.

The door was old-fashioned and without visor, in keeping with the decor of the *Albergo Palazzo*. Horsten opened it and looked out, politely inquisitive.

Two stood there. It took a moment for Helen and her supposed father to recognize them. They had changed from their uniforms into very formal looking clothing. They were two of Chief Customs Inspector Grossi's men.

Horsten frowned. "Yes?"

They bowed formally. "The Signore Juarez is without doubt here?"

Helen stuck a thumb in her mouth. "You mean my boyfriend Zorro?" she said around it.

"That will be all, dear," Horsten said. Then to the newcomers, "Why, yes. Citizen Juárez is here."

The other one spoke, his voice as formal as his partner's. "We call on a matter of honor," he announced. "Undoubtedly, the Signore Juarez will have someone to act for him."

PART TWO

V

DR. DORN HORSTEN looked at the newcomers. "Matter of honor?" he repeated.

The committee bowed with fine formality.

He who had spoken first said, "The inspector is desolated, Signore. He realized, only after the departure of Signore Juarez that he had practically given the lie to the Signore's claim to gentle blood upon the planet of his origin, the status of, uh, Gentleman Gaucho."

Helen caught on first. "You mean," she said, "that silly inspector wants to doodle my Zorro?"

The two stood stiffly, looking straight ahead.

Horsten muttered, "Zen!"

The second customs man said, "Perhaps the Code Duello differs somewhat on Vacamundo. Suffice to say that our custom has it that choice of weapons, place and time of meeting is to be set by the Signore challenged and to be arranged by the respective seconds of the Signori involved."

The algae specialist said hurriedly, "Now, see here. Perhaps this can all be settled without further difficulty."

The two eyed him coldly.

Helen said, "Why don't you go home?"

The first said, "Perhaps the Signore Juarez should, at this point, name the seconds he wishes to represent him."

Horsten thought about it quickly. "Look," he said. "Wait here a minute." He turned and strode back to the living room.

"What's up?" Jerry said from where he slouched in a comfort chair.

Horsten looked at Zorro. "The inspector has been thinking it over. He's decided he insulted you, by impugning your status as a Gentleman Gaucho, or whatever you are when you carry one of those hide-away whips."

Zorro looked at him. "My tranca? They're nothing. Everybody carries one. I made it up as I went along."

"Great. Well, now you're stuck with the story."

Zorro grunted irritation. "Then just tell him I accept his apology."

"He isn't apologizing, exactly. He's sent two of his men as seconds. Evidently, he figures that not to offer you a chance to clobber him is a reflection on the Firenze code of honor."

Zorro was flabbergasted. "What do we do now?"

Jerry said, "Refuse him, and you lose face, or image, or whatever it is you lose when you back down before a challenge."

Horsten said, "You're supposed to be a rough and tough cattleman, here to do business. Your cover will be under suspicion if you try to wiggle out, particularly after that haughty Gentleman Gaucho show you put on."

Zorro said disgustedly, "What do they want right now?"

"For you to name two seconds, to get together with them and arrange for the duel."

"All right, so you're my seconds. Go make a date to confer with them and we'll figure out what to do later."

"Are you sure that's what you want?"

"What else can we do, damn it?"

Jerry got to his feet. "There ought to be some pun I could make on the fact that I've never been a second before, always first."

"Very funny," Zorro growled.

Horsten and Jerry Rhodes went back to the entry.

Helen was standing there, hands on hips, eyeing the two customs men dangerously. "I'm not going to let that silly inspector hurt my Uncle Zorro," she was telling them.

Their faces were pained, but they did their best to maintain dignity.

Horsten said, "Helen, do be quiet. This is adult business."

"Ha!" Helen snorted.

He said to the two, "Citizen Rhodes and I have been named seconds for Citizen Juarez. I suggest we meet tonight in the hotel bar. I assume there is a hotel bar?"

There was a hotel bar.

"At say, ten o'clock?"

Ten o'clock that night in the hotel bar was acceptable. They bowed.

Dr. Horsten bowed.

Jerry Rhodes bowed.

Helen stuck out her tongue.

When the seconds of Chief Customs Inspector Grossi had gone, Horsten said, after a long thoughtful moment, "I hope this is what it looks to be on the surface," he said.

"How's that?" Jerry asked him.

"Is it simply the sort of nonsense that would prevail under any society that allowed an anachronism such as dueling? Or, is Zorro being deliberately eliminated by someone—perhaps the Engelists? Remember Bulchand?"

"Bulchand?" Helen said.

"The Section G agent formerly stationed here. He was challenged and killed."

Jerry said, in unwonted seriousness, "You're right. A customs inspector would be in a good position to eliminate an undesirable. He's one of the first to see a newcomer to Firenze. And with an off-beat planet like this, how many newcomers are there that wouldn't pull what amounted to some sort of local boner right off the bat? Enough of a boner so that he could be challenged."

Horsten said, "You think it's a put-up job?"

"It was your idea, and it could be."

Helen said, "Let's get back to Zorro. Mentioning Bulchand brings up the matter of our getting underway."

They went back to the living room where Zorro was discovered mixing himself another drink.

"Everything settled?" he asked.

"We meet them in the bar at ten," Jerry said. Then to Helen, "What do you mean, getting underway?"

Helen resumed her seat, crossed her plump legs and went businesslike. "Our only contact here, since Bulchand is dead, is the office of Section G in the U.P. Embassy, whoever's holding it down. So, let's get around to a visit."

Horsten said, "We can claim we were instructed to report there and register as U.P. citizens from overspace, due to upset conditions prevailing on Firenze."

"What upset conditions?" Helen said.

"The unsettled political situation occasioned by the underground," Horsten said reasonably.

"That makes sense," Zorro said. "If anybody's got any tails following us, we've got a perfect alibi for going to the U.P. offices. I'll phone down to the desk and find out where the embassy is." He put his glass on the bar and went out to the entry hall where there was a phone screen.

Helen tossed back the rest of her drink, with a practiced stiff-wristed motion that made Dorn Horsten grimace. "I wish there was some way you could wear adult clothing when we were alone," he complained. "Perhaps you'd look like a midget, but at least . . ."

"Knock it, you overgrown lummox. It'd look fine, wouldn't it, if I had a lot of adult clothing tucked away in my luggage for the first snoop to find?"

"Well, at least look as though you're sipping lemonade or something. You give me an ulcer tossing down that hard stuff as though you were practicing for your Interplanetary Alcoholics Anonymous lack-of-merit badge."

Helen snorted contempt of his opinion.

Zorro came back, his face even darker than nature had tinted it.

"What's the matter?" Jerry said, yawning. "I say, let's call off everything and go out on the town. Stretch our legs after that *Half Moon* kettle."

"We might as well," Zorro said. "If the U.P. Embassy was our one contact, then we're contactless."

"What's that supposed to mean?" Helen said.

"The representatives of U.P. on the member planet Firenze have just been sent a-packing," Zorro told her.

"*Why?*" Jerry and Horsten blurted in unison.

"For being, and I quote, a hotbed of subversive activity."

The other three stared at him.

Zorro said, "Whoever it was I was talking to, at the desk, was on the suspicious side that I should even ask about the U.P. Embassy."

Horsten said, "How long's this applied?"

"Evidently, it just happened today. If I got the right impression, the local police caught some of the personnel

52

messing around in internal politics and the whole kit and kaboodle were kicked off the planet."

Helen said, "I told you. These subversives have infiltrated everywhere. They've got to the point where they're about to make their grand play. This planet is going to explode any time. It'll be a madhouse."

"And if it does," Horsten mutterd, "our assignment has failed. And Firenze will be one planet that can be written off for a few years at least, so far as a plus sign is concerned on the balance sheet of the human race's potential."

"It's not necessarily that bad," Jerry said. "Maybe a new government would be better than this present one. The First Signore and his administration seem to spend all their time worrying about the bad guys."

Helen said, contemptuous of that opinion, "That's not the way the Octagon sees it. This planet believes in a liberal progressive policy. It's its tradition, its desire. These damned Engelists are trying to upset the applecart and take over."

Horsten looked at her. "How do you know?"

"Isn't it obvious?" she demanded. "They're trying to undermine a politico-economic system that's trying to be progressive. The only thing that's fouling up Firenze is this underground."

Zorro Juarez had wandered off to a window and was staring out glumly. "You'd think we were in one of those penitentiaries they have in the historical Tri-Di shows," he growled.

Horsten looked over at him. "How do you mean?"

Zorro motioned. "Look at these iron bars at the windows. Strong enough for an elephant's cage. They sure don't want anybody getting in at this First Signore of theirs."

The scientist came over. "Hmm," he hmmed. He looked down. The *Albergo Palazzo* was some ten stories high. "Huh," he grunted.

"Oh, oh," Helen said.

Zorro looked at Helen, and then at Dorn Horsten. "What's the matter?"

Horsten said, "See here, how long is that bullwhip of yours?"

"A little over twenty feet. Why?"

The algae specialist peered down some more. "Because somebody's got to go over to the U.P. Embassy and get into the Section G files on Firenze and the Engelists. I never met Bulchand, but I've heard about him. He was a good man. He must have made *some* progress."

53

Jerry Rhodes said, "I seem to be missing something. What goes on?"

Helen was far ahead of him. "Possibly the Engelists are keeping an eye on us. For all we know, they're aware of the fact that we're from Section G. If they've infiltrated the local United Planets Embassy, they might even have agents back on Earth, right in the Octagon." She looked at Dorn Horsten. "Which brings up a matter we can dwell on later. How do we know this subversive underground applies only here on Firenze?"

Jerry said plaintively, "You're getting more complicated by the minute. What are you two talking about?"

Helen said, "One of us, at least, has got to get over to that U.P. Embassy and get Bulchand's files. But we've got to do it in such a way that we're not suspected, by either the Engelists, on the off chance they're watching us, or by Maggiore Verona and his Anti-Subversion department."

Zorro said, "Why do we have to worry about the maggiore?"

Horsten said, "Isn't it obvious? These people see an Engelist behind every tree. If friend Verona suspects us of hanky-panky the least he'd do would be to expel us from Firenze."

Helen said, "So what it sums up to is that somebody's got to leave this hotel without being spotted, get to the U.P. Embassy without being spotted, search the Section G office, and get back here—without being spotted."

"Makes sense," Jerry wailed. "We don't even know where the U.P. Embassy is. And so far as getting out of this hotel without being spotted is concerned, the only way out is the elevator and through the front lobby. This damn hotel was obviously designed so that the guests were as conspicuous as a walrus in a goldfish bowl."

Horsten had turned back to the iron barred windows. Thoughtfully, he reached out, grasped two of the bars and flexed his arms. The bars bent, bow-shaped, until there was sufficient room between them for . . .

"Oh no," Jerry complained. "I'm lucky, maybe, but not *that* lucky."

Zorro said suspiciously, "Why'd you want to know how far my bullwhip'd reach?"

Helen chuckled and went over to her hatbox of toys. She began to stir around in it. "Where's my brass knucks?" she muttered.

Dorn Horsten said to Jerry Rhodes, "You go down to

the lobby and get a map of this town from the concierge. They must have some facilities for tourists. You might prattle with him for awhile on a sightseeing tour of the city. At any rate, locate some sort of map of Firenze. The only requirement is that it shows where the U.P. building is located."

Zorro said, "Hold on a minute. You and Helen seem to have some sort of telepathic rapport, but I'd like to know what's developing."

Helen had come to her feet and was deftly twisting one of her toys about. Part of it fell away, and she tossed that portion back into the hatbox, humming, *"Two little girls in blue, tra la."* She fitted the remaining part to the knuckles of her right hand and tested the device by banging it into the palm of her left hand with an air of fine competence. She looked at the Vacamundo cattleman.

"Smarten up, lover. Dorn and Jerry are due to go down to the bar at ten o'clock to arrange for you being skewered by the inspector. They'll distract any attention that might be focused on our party. Any tails, either Engelist or government, will stick to them. We'll be left up here. Me to go to bed with my dolly, you to be sitting around in a tizzy, wondering about your duel."

"I don't think I like this," Zorro began.

"What in the name of the Holy Ultimate is that?" Zorro growled at his pint-sized companion.

"A slingshot," Helen said. She stuck her pink tongue out the right side of her mouth, closed one eye and drew a bead. She let loose and something went *ping* and the light immediately below them went out.

"Suppose somebody comes to repair that?"

"By then, we'll be gone. Come on, lover."

Muttering, Zorro Juarez twisted the tip of his whip about the leg of a stone gargoyle, which overlooked the ledge upon which they stood, and gave it a double tug. Helen grabbed him by the belt, gave herself a swing, and landed up on his shoulder.

"Hey," he said.

She ignored him.

He gave the leather thong another tug and then swung himself over the side and began the way down, hand over hand, his feet braced against the wall.

"How the devil did Horsten know I'd done any mountain climbing?" he growled, as though not expecting an answer.

Helen was hanging onto his neck. She said sweetly, "Oh, the doctor is less absentminded than he projects, and not nearly so nice. Neither am I, for that matter."

He grunted at that.

"We both went over your dossier very thoroughly before we started on this assignment." She giggled. "*We* know why you had to leave Vacamundo. Aren't you ashamed?"

Even as they descended, his body stiffened. "*What!*"

They had reached the next terrace level. The last couple of feet, Zorro Juarez had to drop.

"Sh," Helen said. She looked at him from the side of her eyes. "That was a shot in the dark," she murmured. "Kind of a gag. Why *did* you have to leave Vacamundo?"

Zorro snorted, even as he flicked his whip in such wise that the tip, up above, disengaged itself from the gargoyle's leg. "None of your business," he growled. "Besides, I didn't have to leave."

"Ha," Helen sneered.

He peered over the balustrade of the terrace. "From now on down, it's straight wall," he said.

"Only three floors. A cinch."

"A cinch! And how in hell do we get back up, even if we ever get down without breaking our fool necks?"

She was looking down as well. "No problem. We lower ourselves to the next window. We hang on there until you can attach that fancy whip of yours to the bars. Then down to the next window. Only three floors." She looked at him mockingly. "Not afraid, are you, big boy?"

He shot a dark look at her, and began to arrange the whip they were using as a rope, once again. "How I ever got myself talked into taking this job . . ." he muttered.

This time, she swung up onto his back and held her chubby arms and legs around neck and waist. "Let's get going," she said. "Dorn and Jerry will stretch it out, but we should be back by the time they've finished arranging for your demise at the hands of the inspector. Everything will look very authentic if we're there to welcome them at the door when they return, or at least if you are. Properly, eight-year-old Helen would be in bed."

He stared down the next twenty feet of wall. "If somebody sees us at one of these windows," he growled, "they'll figure we're vampires trying to get in."

At the ground floor, they were in an alley behind the *Albergo Palazzo*. They stood for a moment, after Zorro had disengaged his whip, gathering themselves.

56

He looked up from whence they had come and shuddered.

Helen said cheerfully, "What an alibi. There's not a judge in the Confederation who could be talked into believing that anybody'd gotten out of the hotel that way."

A voice rumbled, "Who's there! Stand quietly! I've been watching. You're covered with a scrambler. Don't move!"

Zorro muttered a curse of despair.

Helen squealed, "Save me! Save me! I'm being kidnapped!" and with her arms spread wide, scooted in the direction of the voice, in the shadows of the narrow way.

She was within a few feet of the unknown before she made out his figure.

"Look out!" the other yelped, even as she flung herself into his arms. He was uniformed, brawny, and, right now, completely dismayed. He tried to extricate his gun hand from the crying, obviously terrified child.

"Let go!" he demanded desperately.

"I want my daddy!" she shrilled. "I'm being kidnapped!"

The officer tried to get his gun hand again.

A thong reached out and plucked the weapon, all but gently, from his hand. There was a sigh of leather again hissing through the air.

"Save me, save me!" Helen was squealing.

But now there was no answer, the other's breath being cut off very effectively indeed by the thong around his neck. He could feel the black ebbing in, and his last thoughts were of absolute disbelief.

Helen and Zorro stood above him, moments later, staring down in consideration.

Zorro muttered, "I'd better finish him."

Helen looked up, startled. "What!"

He glared at her. "Well, what else? You want to leave him here? He'll wake in a few minutes. He's only passed out from lack of oxygen."

"You can't kill him!"

He looked at her, half belligerently, half in surprise. "Why not? He's expendable, isn't he? If there was anything Sid Jakes and Lee Chang Chu drilled into us, it was how big the issues are. How many Section G operatives cash in each year?"

"You've got your values a little twisted, lover," Helen told him. "This Section G operative, at least, doesn't slit the throat of the first half-baked cop that gets in her way, just to keep the trail neat. Among other things, he's on our side, he's no Engelist. Besides, we've got other resources."

She unsnapped a pin from her bib-like apron, twisted the end neatly and, with the point, scratched the back of the hand of the fallen man. He was already beginning to groan, his air coming back to him.

"Lucky I brought along this memory-wash hypo," she muttered. "We're really using it."

Zorro stared down at the fallen guard. "And what happens when his relief, or his superior, or whoever, finds him with three hours of memory gone?"

Helen shrugged, replacing the disguised hypodermic needle. "Who knows?" she said. "Possibly we'll come to that bridge."

"Probably, you mean," he said sourly. "Let's get out of here."

They had memorized the map which Jerry Rhodes had gotten at the hotel desk. It had been one of those as near foolproof as possible, charts of a city which are handed out to travelers of any age, in any nation, on any planet where the *genus* tourist may be anticipated. And the U.P. building had, happily, been located but a few blocks from the city's most deluxe hotel, the *Albergo Palazzo*. All of which wasn't too surprising, both edifices being located in the most swank area of the city.

There were at least fifteen men stationed outside the former headquarters of the United Planets. Some ten of them were in uniform, at least six carrying muffle rifles; the other four, evidently officers, were armed with hand-weapons in quick-draw holsters. The rest of the Florentines were plainclothesmen.

Zorro and Helen passed on the opposite side of the street, she holding his hand and skipping along. Zorro hissed, "How in the name of Holy Jumping Zen are we supposed to get past that army?"

"*Three little girls in blue, tra la.*"

"Shut up," he growled.

When they were well past the building in question, they stopped in a shadow and looked back. "Out of the question," he said.

"You know," Helen said slowly. "The way they look, I get the feeling the building hasn't been searched yet. They must have gone through all the gobbledygook of ordering the U.P. personnel off the planet, and such, late enough in the day that they've postponed until tomorrow getting into the archives."

"Maybe, but so what? A mouse couldn't get through that guard."

58

"We're not mice," Helen muttered. "Haven't you noticed? Both sides and the back are surrounded by park. Very formal, very natty, very swank. The United Planets have an impressive building as an Embassy."

He was contemptuous. "You think there wouldn't be an equivalent guard at the back door?"

"I don't believe in doors," Helen told him. "Come on, let's check out that park. There'll probably be lovers in there, and an occasional drunk sprawled on a bench. A man taking his daughter for a walk won't look off-beat."

Zorro said nothing. He grabbed up her hand and started for the parkgrounds, grumbling under his breath.

"Easy lover, easy," Helen said in her childish treble. "Us eight-year-olds aren't up to your pace."

They circled the building without being intercepted. They spotted at least two or three plainclothesmen wandering the park paths, but none looked at the pair twice. There were also half a dozen armed men at the rear entry.

"Well," Zorro said, complete with sarcasm. "Satisfied?"

"Sure," she said. "Did you notice that open window on the second floor, back in that nice shady corner?"

"No."

"Well, come on."

They found the corner in question and stationed themselves beneath the shelter of a tree.

Zorro looked up and shook his head in negation. "I couldn't get through there, even if we could get up."

"Nobody asked you to," Helen said tartly. "Can you latch onto something up there, with that whip of yours?"

He looked down at her. "I can try. What do you have in mind?" He looked around, unbuttoned his jerkin and unwound his whip from about his waist.

"Going in, of course."

He flicked the whip and the end reached up, sought, fell back again. She stood there, hands on hips, impatiently—for all the world, a precocious eight-year-old.

"Alone?" he said, unbelievingly. The thong reached up again, fell back.

She snorted, not bothering to answer.

He tried for a full five minutes. "No go," he said finally, an element of relief in his voice. "There's nothing to hook onto."

"All right," she said. "Can you toss me up?"

He stared at her. "What?"

She said impatiently, "You've seen me work out with Dorn in the gym. I said, can you toss me up?"

He turned his stare to the small window in question. "I could try, but suppose I missed and you fell?"

"Then catch me, you zany!"

He reached down doubtfully, to take her by the waist.

"Not that way, stupid. Here." She showed him how to grasp her.

A moment later, she was hanging onto the window ledge. Without looking back, she gracefully pulled herself up and disappeared within. Zorro stared for a moment, muttered something, then sank back further into the shadow of the tree.

He agonized there for a full fifteen minutes. By that time, he was nervously shooting glances up and down the park walk. It was becoming obvious to him that something had happened to her. What? What could he do? He swore impotently under his breath. And if a guard came along, what could he do? It was one thing, strolling along through the park with a child by the hand. It was another, sulking beneath this tree.

He heard a hiss and looked up.

"Catch me!" she called, and, without further ado, launched herself into space.

He got his arms up, just in time. She landed in them lightly; more lightly than even the cubic content of her tiny body seemed to call for.

"What happened?" he growled. "Where in the hell were you so long? I thought you were simply getting the layout, trying to figure out some way of getting in."

"I *was* in," she said, disengaging herself from him and straightening her short skirt, in a prissy, childlike gesture. "I had to locate the Section G offices."

"How did you possibly do that, in a building that size?"

"Oh, I found a nightguard."

He stared down at her, even as he grabbed one of her hands and began hustling her toward the nearest walk. Just as he was about to blurt another query, two figures loomed before them. One of the newcomers had his hand on his holstered handweapon.

"What were you doing back in those shadows!" one demanded.

Helen looked up demurely. "I had to do wee wee," she said. She continued on, not looking back, hauling Zorro by the hand. He thanked whatever gods might be around that he had rewrapped the whip about his waist.

They could hear the Florentines continuing on their way. Zorro breathed deeply.

He said, finally, "What'd you mean, you found a guard? What'd he do to you? How'd you get away?"

"Oh, *I* didn't get away. But he tried to," she said with an air of deprecation. She cleared her throat slightly. "I had to, uh, coax him a little, but he told me where the Section G office was."

Zorro Juarez rolled his eyes upward in agony. "They'll be on us like a ton of beef! Verona's security cops will . . ."

"Don't be silly," she said. "You think that bully-boy, when he regains consciousness . . ."

"Consciousness," he repeated weakly.

". . . is going to repeat a story like that to his superior officer? That a child came up and tortured him into giving some answers?"

"I give up," he said. "Don't tell me any more. No, wait. What did you find in Bulchand's files, in the Section G office?"

"Nothing."

"Nothing!"

"Nothing at all. The files had been ransacked."

VI

"RANSACKED?" Dorn Horsten said. "You mean, Maggiore Verona's anti-subversive men had already been there?"

They were back in the penthouse suite of the *Albergo Palazzo*, the three men standing around Helen, an enormous highball glass in her right hand.

"Ransacked," she repeated. "And by the looks of the place, not necessarily by the authorities. It had a look of too much confusion. Whoever went through that office was in a hurry."

"You found nothing at all?" Jerry Rhodes said. "Golly, that's awful luck."

"Yeah," she snarled. "It's too bad you weren't there."

"Um," he said absently.

"*You* would have found the minutes of the last meeting of the executive committee of the Engelists, or something."

"Possibly not that," he admitted, the sarcasm passing him by.

"I oughta slug you," she snarled.

"Easy, easy," Horsten muttered. "That leaves us absolutely nowhere, and with nowhere to go. Obviously . . ."

"Obviously, somebody else got to the Section G files first, and now we're completely on our own," Zorro growled. "Well, I'm off to bed. Can any of you imagine what's involved in climbing up this hotel wall? All the way to the penthouse, floor by floor, half the time hooking onto something above with my whip, half the time heaving this little brat up ahead to attach the whip. I'll tell you . . ."

"Knock it," Helen said. "It was fun."

He rolled his eyes upward and left for his room.

"That reminds me," Horsten said. He went over to the window the two had used for exit and reentry and bent the heavy iron bars back into their original position.

Jerry shook his head. "I wish I could do that," he marveled.

Helen said, "Why don't you just bet somebody a stick of gum that you could? Then this fabulous luck of yours would come to the rescue, and you'd do it."

He looked at her. "You're beginning to get the idea."

Helen snorted.

Zorro stuck his head back through the door of his bedroom and called to Horsten, "By the way, how did you manage to squash that duel thing?"

"We didn't."

"What!"

"You're scheduled for the day after tomorrow—we couldn't postpone it any longer—in the *Parco Duello*, at dawn."

"Oh, fine. A great couple of seconds, you two are. Why didn't you apologize?"

"How could we apologize?" Jerry said reasonably. "*You* hadn't done anything."

Horsten said, "We've got two days to figure something out. We'll check with Maggiore Verona. There's undoubtedly some manner in which to duck out of a duel."

"Do you mind telling me what kind of weapon you decided to let me get killed with?"

Horsten said, "Well, we should have checked with you on that. We didn't know what you were handy with—besides a bullwhip."

"So . . . ?"

"So we chose swords."

"Wonderful! I've never had a sword in my hand in my life." Zorro slammed the door behind him.

They had a glum breakfast together.

Zorro, in a foul humor, complained, "Why'd they send

us off from the Octagon with no more to work on than this? We should have been given some sort of lead, some sort of takeoff point."

Helen said, "For one thing, Ross Metaxa doesn't want us to succeed."

Dorn Horsten looked at her, between bites of toast, his eyebrows high.

Helen said, "The Special Talents group is a pet of Lee Chang's but Metaxa doesn't like it. It louses up the atmosphere of dignity he'd like to associate with his beloved Section G."

Jerry Rhodes said, "He's the boss. Why not just eliminate us special talents agents?"

"Because Lee Chang's one of his favorite supervisors and one of his best. He can't just slap her down. Besides, Sid Jakes more or less backs her project."

Horsten said, "Then you think if we flunk this assignment, Lee Chang's whole idea will go by the board?"

Helen sipped her pseudo-coffee. "Of course. That was the arrangement."

Zorro growled, "You wonder what side Ross Metaxa is on. But what gets me is we're evidently expendable. It's all fine for him, sitting there in the Octagon waiting for us to blow this job and get ourselves killed off in duels so he can prove a point to Lee Chang and Jakes. So to accomplish it, we get insufficient material with which to work."

Horsten said uncomfortably, "We don't know that's true. The situation is unique. Bulchand was the sole Section G agent, and he was killed and his files taken. Ross Metaxa had nothing to do with all that. Don't be bitter, Zorro."

Helen smeared jam on her toast to a thickness that made her supposed father wince. "I hate a bitter man," she said.

Jerry Rhodes said, "I bitter woman, once."

Zorro, his mouth tightly shut, came to his feet and threw his napkin to the table. He glared around at them, then turned and left the room abruptly.

Jerry said to his remaining two companions, "Sorry. I guess I'm not as funny as I think I am."

The scientist pushed his pince-nez back to a more comfortable spot on his nose and said, "He's got that confounded duel on his mind. He doesn't want to kill that inspector—he has no reason to—and, on the other hand, doesn't want to get killed himself."

Helen shrugged tiny shoulders. "Maybe. However, I'm beginning to get the impression that friend Zorro figures everybody is expendable but Zorro."

Horsten looked at her. "You two have a run-in?"

"Not particularly. He's just a bit on the cold-blooded side for little Helen."

Dorn Horsten said, "Remember, he's part of the team. His being around might mean the difference between your neck and its wringing, someday." He looked at his watch and switched subjects. "We're going to have to get some lead on this underground outfit. The desk phoned a little while ago and I have an appointment to meet Academician Udine from the university. He's not a complete stranger; we met during my past brief visit here. It comes to mind that he will undoubtedly feel more at ease with me, than with a fellow citizen of Firenze. Perhaps I can draw him out."

"On the Engelists, eh?" Helen said.

"Uh huh. If there's this much underground activity on Firenze, then the universities should be hotbeds of subversion. It's when man is young and idealistic that he rebels against the status quo."

Jerry said, "If rebellion is called for or not?"

Helen finished off her pseudo-coffee. "Jerry, my lad, rebellion against the status quo is almost always called for. A culture shouldn't be allowed to become static. Wasn't it that old-timer Thomas Jefferson who thought they ought to have a new revolution about every twenty years?"

Jerry grunted. "Then why're we here on Firenze trying to foul up these Engelists?"

Dorn Horsten came to his feet. "Because they're a little too previous. It's not as though the present government is in decadence. It's never been allowed to get underway. They want to be progressive, but this confounded underground won't let them get started."

He looked at his wrist chronometer again. "At any rate, I'll see if I can get a line on the Engelists through my colleague Udine."

"How about me?" Helen said.

He scowled at her. "I can't take you along. He wouldn't open up in front of a child. He'd think you couldn't be trusted not to repeat something."

Jerry said, "Helen and I can go out on the town and find what we can find. Possibly, we'll be lucky and stumble on something. Suppose we meet back here for lunch."

"What's happened to Zorro?"

"Who knows?" Helen said. "I heard the door open and close a few minutes ago."

"For lunch it is, then," the massive scientist said, leaving them.

When he was gone, Jerry and Helen sat alone. Helen looked at him unblinkingly for a long moment.

Finally he began to get apprehensive. "You're going to come up with something," he accused.

She said, "I'll bet you a hundred interplanetary credits."

"On what?"

"What do you care? You said you always win a bet."

"All right, all right. I always win a bet, but one of the reasons I do is that I don't push it beyond reason. I wouldn't bet, for instance, that I could be in two places at once."

"Trying to crab out, eh?"

"What's the bet?"

Helen said slowly, "I'll bet you one hundred credits that Zorro gets killed in that duel."

He said finally, "All right. I'll bet you a hundred he doesn't."

At the desk, in the lobby of the *Albergo Palazzo,* Jerry Rhodes, the look of a martyr on his face, stopped long enough to say to the concierge, "Look, for this morning I'm saddled with a babysitting routine, understand? But I'd appreciate it if you'd make arrangements for me tonight. A limousine, some suggestions for nightspots. You know, where the action . . ."

"Nightspots?" the concierge said.

Jerry, who had Helen firmly by the hand as he talked, said, aggrieved, "Nightspots, nightspots, whatever you call them on Firenze. Cabaret, *café dansant,* music hall, nightclub." As the other's face remained blank, his voice went pleading. ". . . saloon, gin mill, pub, *bistro,* beer hall . . ." The other's face was still blank. ". . . speakeasy! blind tiger!"

The clerk held up a hand to stem the tide. "I know what you mean. But the curfew."

It was Jerry's turn to be blank. "Curfew?"

"Let's go, Uncle Jerry," Helen whined, pulling at his hand. She had her doll under her left arm.

The concierge said, "At ten o'clock, all public establishments must be closed. At eleven o'clock, all citizens must be off the streets."

Jerry said, *"Why?"*

The clerk's face and voice turned cool. "Signore, are you criticizing the measures taken by the First Signore and his Council of Signori?"

"No. Why?"

The concierge looked left and right, as though in sub-conscious check. He leaned a bit over the desk, and his tone was lower. "It seems that the Fifth Signore recommended to the First Signore, that the nightspots, as you call them, be temporarily closed. Evidently, they were being used as drops by the underground."

Jerry groaned. "How long ago did that happen?" he said.

Helen whined, "Uncle Jerry, let's go. You promised me and Gertrude a ice cream."

The concierge said, "Why, actually, before my time. The curfew has been in effect for years."

"Swell!" Jerry muttered. He gave Helen's arm a tug as he started for the door, still muttering.

Out on the street, he said, in disgust, "No nightclubs, and me with an unlimited expense account and with the job of projecting myself as a playboy."

Helen said sweetly, "You seem to have terrible luck, Uncle Jerry, old boy, old lad. Maybe that coin is beginning to flip tails."

He snorted contempt of that opinion.

"Where're we going?" he said.

"How would I know? To case this town." They were walking down the avenue, obviously one of the city's best, and heading toward the main shopping district. Helen stared at a window devoted to fashions.

Jerry jerked her arm. "Watch yourself," he said from the side of his mouth. "You're supposed to be interested in toy shops, ice cream parlors and such, not *haute couture.*"

Helen grunted sourly, but, to project her character, began to skip.

Her supposed guardian for the morning was taking in their fellow pedestrians and the passing traffic. He said softly, for her ears alone, "I thought Metaxa said this was potentially one of the more advanced worlds. It looks a few centuries behind the times to me. And nine people out of ten look on the raggedy side."

She said, "I get the same impression. However, that's the point. The underground's got things so fouled up that the progressive elements can't get underway."

Jerry Rhodes spotted a sidewalk café.

He said, "What'd you say we sit down and let the town come to us? Have a mead, or something."

She smiled up at him with the trustfulness of an eight-year-old in the hands of a mature adult, but her voice

66

held a low snarl. "Mead, you rat. You know damn well I won't be able to order anything stronger than lime squash."

"Oh, that's right." He grinned down at her. "Sorry. You feel the need to kill the hangover? You were really knocking them back last night."

"I'll kill *you,* if you don't knock that condescending tone in your silly voice." She grunted satisfaction as they got nearer to the sidewalk café. The place was packed. Obviously, in view of the night curfew, the citizens of Firenze were forced to do their imbibing early in the day.

"No tables," she said. "So you'll do without, too."

"Oh, we ought to be lucky enough to find something," Jerry murmured, heading for the more preferable locations.

"With all these people standing around waiting for a table?" she said nastily.

However, at that split second, three Florentines came to their feet, one looking at his wrist chronometer apprehensively. They hurried off.

"Here we are," Jerry beamed, pulling back a chair and then taking her up from behind by the elbows and sitting her down.

"Talk about *luck . . ."* she began, and then shut her mouth to glare at him.

He turned to take a chair of his own, only to find it occupied.

The stranger looked up. "I got here first," he said.

Jerry took him in for a long moment, finally saying bitterly, "You want us to leave?"

The other waved a nonchalant hand. "Not at all, not at all. Strangers to Firenze?" He indicated the table's third chair. "Be my guest."

Jerry Rhodes sat down. "You have to be speedy in this town, don't you?"

"Well, Signore, I'll tell you . . ." But then the other, as though suddenly remembering the amenities, came to his feet, brought his heels together and bowed stiffly. "May I introduce myself? The Great Marconi."

Helen had leaned her elbows on the tabletop, her chin in her cupped hands. She stared at him unblinkingly. "You don't look so great," she told him. "You oughta see my daddy."

The Great Marconi put his right hand to his heart and bowed again, more sweepingly. "Signorina, you convince me. I am most certain your parent is even greater than the Great Marconi."

"Betcha boots," Helen informed him ungraciously.

Jerry Rhodes came to his feet in turn, clicked his heels and bowed. "The pleasure is ours," he said. "And I am the Great Rhodes, and this is the Great Helen."

The other sank back into his chair and looked at Jerry speculatively. "You condescend with me?" he said. "You jest?"

"Who me?" Jerry said in disgust. "Be condescending? I wouldn't dare. Although all sorts of puns and such come to mind. I could've introduced myself as Cross Rhodes, the guy who becomes slightly sore when somebody slips into his chair, right under him. And I could have pointed out Miss Horsten here"—he indicated Helen—"and said, 'She looks like Helen Brown, but her real name is Horsten, and she looks cute in blue.' "

Helen's face was pained. "I betcha I could think of a funnier one than that."

The Great Marconi evidently couldn't decide whether to laugh or mount higher into the saddle of dignity. He said evenly, "You are undoubtedly unacquainted with Firenze usage, Signore."

"Undoubtedly," Jerry said, looking about for a waiter, half a dozen of whom were scooting around amidst the tables.

Their unwelcome Florentine companion evidently couldn't help putting in a dig. He said, "To get a waiter's attention here at the Florida Café, you'd have to have the luck of . . ."

He broke it off.

A waiter had magically materialized at the elbow of Jerry Rhodes.

"Ha!" Helen said under her breath.

Jerry said, "One ice cream and—you do have ice cream on this planet? Nobody's decided it's subversive, or something?"

The waiter looked at him. "Are you criticizing the . . ."

But Jerry had held up a hand in horror. "Certainly not!" He looked at the self-named Great Marconi. "What's a good morning pick-me-up on this planet?"

"Try a Grappa Sour," the other said, and then to the waiter, "Two Grappa Sours."

"Three," Helen said.

Jerry and the Great Marconi looked at her. Jerry shook his head. "Ice cream," he said.

The waiter left.

Helen and Jerry turned their eyes to their uninvited companion. He was possibly in his early thirties, lithe of

68

build, quick of movement. His eyes were, if anything, overly bright in a face that fell into a drawn seriousness when relaxed, which was seldom. The Great Marconi was great for moues, smiles, animated grimaces; it was as though he wore a mask over a mask. His clothing, while not as seedy as that of many of his fellow Florentines, could have used a bit of spotting up. He hadn't exactly slept in them, but . . .

He bore their scrutiny.

Helen said finally, "What makes you great, Mr. the Great Marconi?"

"Yeah," Jerry said ungraciously. "You an unemployed magician, or something?" Then, without waiting for an answer, "What're they doing with live waiters on Firenze? I thought the only place you ever saw waiters anymore were in the historical Tri-Di shows, or backward planets such as Goshen, where they've got a feudalistic socioeconomic system."

"You seem to be somewhat critical of our institutions, Signore Rhodes. You're fortunate someone hasn't called you out, as a result. Florentines are touchy in matters of honor."

"Jerry's lucky," Helen said flatly. "Anybody who called him out would probably wind up with laryngitis."

The Great Marconi blinked at her. "What?" he said. It hadn't been exactly the sort of crack that usually comes from a child.

Helen brought the eight-year-old back into play. "Why're you so great?" she said. "My daddy's bigger'n you."

The waiter brought their order. Helen looked in disgust at the ice cream. "A lot of guano for the condors," she muttered.

The Florentine blinked again. "What did you say?"

Jerry covered quickly. "You and Gertrude eat your ice cream, Helen. I'll hear you recite your lessons later."

He took a swallow of his drink, put the glass down and stared into it accusingly. He looked at the Great Marconi. "You people drink this for a pick-me-up? Where I come from, we'd call it a lay-me-down-flat."

The other sipped his own in satisfaction. "Ah. Wonderful," he sighed. Then to Jerry, "Thank you."

"Thank you? For what?" Jerry said. He pushed the glass to one side in rejection.

"For the drink." The Great Marconi beamed at him.

"A free loader," Helen muttered, reaching surreptitiously for Jerry's glass.

Jerry Rhodes looked at the Great Marconi. "You know,"

he said. "Something has just occurred to me. We set down only yesterday, and I haven't gotten around to acquiring a Firenze crediter. Will my Interplanetary do?"

"What's a crediter?" the Great Marconi said, taking another pull at his Grappa Sour.

"A crediter, a crediter," Jerry said. "A credit card, an exchange card, a debenture I.D. What do you call them on this planet?"

The other was looking at him blankly. "I don't know what you're talking about."

Jerry said impatiently, "What do I pay for this drink with?"

"With money," the Florentine said.

"You mean actual money?"

"It'd better not be counterfeit."

Jerry said, "Hey!" and grabbed his drink back from Helen. "You're too young for that kind of stuff."

"Oooo," Helen said. "That's strong." The glass was almost empty.

The Great Marconi stared at her, took in the glass. "You'd better get her back to your hotel. Grappa Sours are sold only one to the customer. They're potent."

Jerry began to growl, "You don't know this . . ." but then cut it short, to cover. He cleared his throat, glared at Helen and said, "I suppose you're right. Since I don't have any of the local exchange, can you pay for this?"

"No."

Jerry looked at him.

The other said, "I thought it was on you."

"You're great, all right," Helen muttered.

He smiled winningly at her. "The greatest, Signorina."

Jerry looked around for the waiter, gave up. He snarled, "Listen, you bum, you never did answer my question. Why do you call yourself the Great Marconi?"

The Great Marconi's face lost its amiability. "Because I am the greatest tutor on all Firenze, Signore. Now as to your designation . . ."

Helen said, "Tooter what?"

The Florentine looked at her. "Little Signorina, I have taken a great attraction to you, in spite of the oafishness of your companion with whom I shall deal in a moment. Any child who can put down a Grappa Sour in a split second . . ." He cleared his throat. "But to answer your question. I tutor gentlemen who have been called out."

His eyes went back to Jerry Rhodes. "I am, without doubt, the greatest fencer, the best shot, on all Firenze."

Jerry snorted disbelief. "Then why're you on your uppers, Citizen Great Marconi? If you were such a stute of a duelist, you'd be on top of the heap. Here, you can't even pay for a couple of drinks."

"An' a ice cream," Helen added for a clincher.

The Great Marconi twisted his expressive face into a moue. "They are afraid to come to me," he admitted. "They should form lines at the door of my studio, but they are afraid."

Jerry and Helen looked at him.

He grunted disgust. "Because I am an Engelist," he said.

"What!" Jerry blurted.

"You wouldn't understand. Local politics."

Jerry Rhodes' usually all but vacuous expression took on a suddenly alert quality. "An Engelist!" he blurted.

Helen grabbed up her doll. "Easy, easy," she crooned. "Take it easy, darling Gertrude."

The Great Marconi said, "You wouldn't understand. As an Engelist, I am a minority element. Very highly discriminated against."

"Of course. Yes, I'm sure," Jerry said, ignoring Helen, who was now kicking him under the table. "Look, I'd like to find out more . . ."

"I feel sick," Helen announced. "I wanna go to my daddy."

"Shut up," Jerry said. Then, back to the Florentine: "Listen, ever since we set down on this planet, we've been hearing about the Engelists, but you're the first one we've met. I'd like a chance, along with some friends, to find out more about your, uh, program and all. How you expect to overthrow the government, and all."

"Oh, you would?"

Helen closed her eyes in mute anguish.

"Yes," Jerry said definitely. "I'd like to know all about it. So would my friends. You'd be surprised." He began looking for the waiter again, snapping his fingers.

"That's interesting," the Great Marconi said, his face expressionless now.

It occurred to Helen that this particular face was more at ease, expressionless, than it was carrying the air of joviality it had up until this point. Inwardly, she groaned. "I wanna go back to my daddy," she bleated.

"Shush," Jerry told her. "As soon as I take care of the bill, we'll all go back to the hotel."

71

She closed her eyes again. "Oh, great. Sucker everybody else in, too."

"What?" the Great Marconi said.

"I said, I wanna go back to my daddy."

The waiter appeared.

Jerry said, "Look, I feel lucky. Tell you what I'll do. We'll flip this coin." He brought his French franc from a pocket. "If I can call it, I don't pay. If I can't, I'll pay you five times the tab."

"Five times?" the waiter said.

"Right."

The waiter said, "It's a deal if you'll let me flip the coin."

"All right. It doesn't make any difference."

The Great Marconi was eyeing Jerry. "What if you lose?" Jerry ignored him, handed the coin to the waiter.

"You'll pay five times the bill?" the waiter said.

"Right," Jerry said impatiently. "Flip it. I want to get going."

The waiter flipped the coin high. While it was still in the air, he called, "Tails!"

The coin hit the table.

Jerry got up without bothering to look, and said to Helen and his newly acquired Engelist friend, "Come on."

The waiter said, "Just a minute. You owe me six and a half silver lire."

"What?" Jerry said.

The waiter pointed.

Jerry Rhodes bug-eyed the coin. He looked up at the waiter blankly. Finally, he got out, "But . . . but I haven't any . . . any money."

"No money!" The other was enraged. "Why, you damned Engelist! Trying to get something for nothing! I took my chance, eh? But you're unable to pay, now you have lost." He spun and yelled, "Gino, Gino! Come here, please. I wish this . . . this *Signore* to be arrested and hauled into the Court of the People! He refuses to pay his bill!"

Jerry Rhodes looked about desperately.

The Great Marconi had disappeared.

VII

DORN HORSTEN peered through the bars. "Where is Helen?" he demanded.

"How would I know?" Jerry growled.

72

Maggiore Roberto Verona, suave as ever, said smoothly, "I am sure the little ragazza is safe. This is all most distressing. What in the world happened, my dear Signore Rhodes?"

Jerry said in exasperation, "Nobody'd listen to me. I forgot to make arrangements for exchange. I didn't know my Interplanetary Crediter wouldn't be legal tender on this half-baked, backward planet."

The maggiore's voice was suddenly chill. "I am sure you are distressed, Signore Rhodes, and shall ignore your derogatory comments." He flicked his hand at a jailer who came forward and opened the cell door.

Dr. Horsten was staring at the accommodations Jerry was departing. "A cell," he exclaimed. "Wonderful. Imagine, in this day and age. A jail. Guards and everything. I can't wait to tell my colleagues on, say, Avalon, or Earth, or . . . well, just about any place."

He turned to Maggiore Verona and beamed. "And my daughter. You have her in, uh, *durance vile*, as well? Oh, wonderful! What an experience." He looked at his disgusted younger colleague. "Jerry, how unfortunate you aren't a journalist, eh? What a story for Interplanetary Press. Ah, tell me again. Just what was this, uh, *romp*, as the gangsters call it on the Tri-Di shows?"

The Florentine official was taken aback. "But, really, Doctor, this is all a terrible misunderstanding. Your daughter . . ."

"Oh, I am sure Helen can take care of herself." Horsten said in growing enthusiasm. "I dote on the historical fiction gangster shows. My only relaxation. I can just see it all. Jerry, here, dashing up in a low-slung, black hovercar. Mufflegun in both hands. Ah, where did it happen, Jerry, my boy?"

"At a sidewalk café," Jerry growled in disgust. "How do we get out of this hole?"

"This way," the maggiore said hastily, trying to stem the universally renowned scientist's tirade.

"Up to the, uh, what do they call them? Pay booth, cash register . . . ?"

The Florentine groaned softly under his breath.

". . . threatening all with his weapon. Dash it, I wish I had been there. Romantic, eh? Jerry, just what was it you did?"

Jerry said sourly, "Couldn't pay my bill. Six and a half silver lire, or whatever. If this ever gets back to Mother, she'll probably buy this town, just to plow it under."

Maggiore Verona looked at him from the side of his eyes, a certain respect there. "Ah, Signori, if you'll just come this way."

He led them down a sterile corridor, the doctor still excitedly proclaiming the romanticism of it all, Jerry scowling darkly. They emerged into a well furnished office in which there were half a dozen Florentines, including two women, obviously matrons by their attire.

Helen was seated on a desk, Gertrude under one arm, holding forth with a highly superior air and a treble voice on the shortcomings of the planet Firenze. Her audience, all in uniform, all on the brawny side—even the feminine contingent—were obviously fascinated.

On spotting her supposed father and his companions, Helen wound it up. "An' when me and Gertrude grow up, if we're still on this dump planet, we're gonna become Engelists."

"What!" the anti-subversion maggiore blurted.

"Me and Gertrude both," Helen said definitely. She looked at her father and switched gears. "I don't like being here," she wailed. "I wanna go home!"

Horsten said hurriedly, "Now, Helen, everything will be all right. We'll return immediately to the hotel."

"I don't wanna go back to that dump hotel. I wanna go home!"

Maggiore Verona was looking bleakly at the Florentines. "What's been going on here?"

One official, who had come suddenly to his feet when the maggiore had entered the room, stuttered an answer. The child had been taken care of with silken gloves. Ice cream had been brought, chocolate for the little girl, strawberry for her doll, who, Helen had claimed, would eat nothing else.

"Very well, very well," Verona finally cut off the tirade. He turned to Horsten and Jerry Rhodes. "My vehicle is waiting. I shall be happy to return you to the hotel, Signori." He looked at Helen, suppressing distaste. "And you too, of course, Signorina."

Helen snorted and tucked Gertrude more firmly under her arm.

On the way back to the *Albergo Palazzo*, the maggiore murmured gently, "Where in the name of the Holy Ultimate would the little ragazza have ever heard of the Engelists? Ah, what sort of conversations do you hold before her?"

"Huh!" Jerry grunted.

"Signore Rhodes?"

Jerry said, "It's the only thing anybody ever talks about on Firenze. Everybody talks about the Engelists, but nobody ever says anything about them. What they stand for, who they are, what they want. I came here to Firenze with the idea of investing some variable capital. But the planet's in a confusion worse than Catalina. I think I'll go back and . . ."

The maggiore said smoothly, "My dear Signore Rhodes, we have checked your credentials, and have also made preliminary investigation of the situation that prevails on your home planet. Tell me, are there others who feel the same way as you do in regard to the, uh, desirability of transferring their investments elsewhere?"

Jerry bent an arrogant glare on him. "I am not sure that is your business, Citizen Verona."

The assistant to the Third Signore contemplated his fingertips. "Only indirectly, Signore. I will be happy to refer you to members of the First Signore's administration who are in a better position to advise you on Firenze investment opportunities. I might say, however, that they are all but unlimited."

"In spite of the Engelists?"

"Perhaps because of them," the other said smoothly. "But here we are at the hotel."

They remained silent until they had regained the penthouse suite usually reserved for the First Signore, now retained by Jerry Rhodes and his guests.

Jerry, projecting a continuation of his indignation over spending an hour or two behind bars, strode immediately toward the bar. He said ungraciously over his shoulder, "Anybody else like a drink?"

Dorn Horsten said, "If you and the maggiore are involved in personal affairs, perhaps I should adjourn. . . ."

"No, stay where you are," Jerry said. "Maybe you'll find out something about this off-beat world, too."

The massive scientist shrugged and settled down in a chair. "Frankly, I am a bit nonplussed," he admitted. "I had been thinking in terms of recommending that an interplanetary research center be established here on Firenze devoted to the *thallophytes*."

The major looked at him. "And . . ."

"Well, one of my local colleagues from the university seemed to differ with my opinions. I answered his objections, but evidently he took umbrage at my vocal inflection."

They were all looking at him.

The algae specialist cleared his throat. "Briefly, he challenged me."

"Challenged you!" Jerry blurted. "Now you?"

"Well, he was a somewhat, shall we say feisty, little fellow. Ah, say, five and a half feet tall or so. He somewhat shrilly called upon me to choose weapons, and when I mentioned the Macedonian sarissa . . ."

"Sarissa?" the maggiore said blankly.

Horsten turned to him and beamed. "The Macedonian phalanx was based on a pike, called the sarissa, which was some twenty feet in length. A conception attributed to Philip. It proved effective."

"Twenty feet?" the major said, still blankly. "And he is five and a half feet tall? A university professor? Could he even pick up such a weapon?"

The doctor's eyes were wide. "I wouldn't think so," he said.

"But . . ."

The doctor spread his hands. "Academician Udine began laughing. Professor Porsena began laughing. Dr. Luna was fractured, I believe is the old idom. Shortly, we were all, uh, in stitches. It eventually came out very nicely."

The maggiore shook his head as though in utter disbelief and turned back to Jerry. "What did you mean, *now you?*"

"Huh?"

"You said, when Dr. Horsten mentioned being challenged, *Now you.*"

"Oh. Zorro Juarez, that cowboy from Vaca. . . . Whatever the name of the place is. He's scheduled to meet the chief customs inspector, Grossi, tomorrow morning at the Parco Duello, wherever that is. The doctor and I are his seconds."

The maggiore said, "No, he's not."

"Yes, he is," Jerry said. "We arranged it, the doctor and I."

The maggiore said, "The Code Duello, on the planet Firenze, applies to signori only. Criminal elements are not eligible to meet on the field of honor. That, of course, includes all subversives such as Engelists."

Helen, who had been following all, wide-eyed, as though understanding only about half of what the adults were saying, said shrilly, "What's that got to do with my Uncle Zorro? Me and Gertrude's gonna marry Uncle Zorro."

They ignored her, but nevertheless, the question was answered.

The maggiore said, "Zorro Juarez has been arrested as a suspected Engelist. As such, he is not eligible to the honor of being called out under the Code Duello."

"You mean he's not allowed to duel tomorrow morning?" Jerry demanded.

"That is correct."

"But what did my Uncle Zorro do?" Helen wailed.

"Yes, what did he do?" Dorn Horsten said.

The major said, "He went into the public library and attempted to secure books on the Engelists."

The otherworldlings stared at him.

The maggiore elaborated patiently: "He conducted himself ridiculously. How he expected to elude the Anti-Firenze Activities officers I couldn't say. He went into the main branch of the city library and asked for books, pamphlets, tapes, or whatever might be available on the Engelist movement."

Jerry said, not quite understanding, "Well, what did they give him?"

"Give him! The librarian he consulted immediately phoned the Bureau of Security and the Anti-Firenze Activities Ministry. He was arrested within moments."

The three looked at him.

"See here. Suppose someone wanted to find out about the Engelists. How would he go about it?" Horsten said.

The maggiore's eyes narrowed. "Why would he want to find out about the Engelists?"

The scientist shrugged. "How would I know? Perhaps he wishes to write a book about them."

"There are already sufficient exposés on the underground traitors, written by competent authorities on the subject."

"Well, why didn't this librarian give them to Citizen Juarez? He obviously was simply curious."

"He didn't want the volumes available. He claimed he wished to consult original sources. He wanted books written by the Engelists themselves!" The maggiore was being patient.

They held another moment of silence.

It was Horsten who took up the ball again. "You mean there is no manner in which a, well, student of the subject can simply go to the public library and take out books about the Engelists, written by Engelists, rather than by their critics?"

It was the major's turn to be bewildered. "Do you think His Zelenza's government is insane?"

Jerry said, "Look. How can anybody combat these subversives if they don't even know what they stand for?"

"We know what they stand for," the maggiore said indignantly.

"What?" Helen said. She was seated on the floor, her hatbox full of toys before her.

Dr. Horsten stepped in quickly. "Out of the mouth of babes, eh?" He chuckled. "But, actually, I have the same question. What do they stand for?"

"Forceable overthrow of the legitimate government and the imposition of a dictatorship!"

"Well, yes, we already gathered that. But how do they expect to go about all this? How do they attempt to appeal to the people? How do they operate?"

The maggiore said, "You seem strangely interested in the Engelists for strangers."

Dorn covered. "Well, it's partly pure curiosity, since we're hearing so much about them. And partly in view of the fact that our companion, poor Zorro, has been arrested as one. All of which seems ridiculous to me. He's never even been on Firenze before. He knows nobody here. Has no interest in your politico-economic system."

The maggiore thought about it. Finally, he said, "Well, here's an example, although I am actually committing an indiscretion." From an inner pocket he drew forth a four page leaflet, printed on cheap paper and, by the looks of it, on some primitive equipment. He handed it over hesitantly to the scientist.

Dorn Horsten scowled down.

"Florentines Arise!" he read. *"Overthrow the Tyranny of Representative Government!"*

"Come again on that one?" Jerry said.

Horsten ignored him and read on. *"Establish the People's Democratic Dictatorship!"*

"It wouldn't really be democratic," the maggiore injected. "All they want is to seize power for themselves."

"Fellow citizens of Firenze, adopt the following program. One. Infiltrate the army and police forces and kill your officers. Two. Boycott the elections. Three. Destroy the machines directed at . . ."

The scientist stopped, flabbergasted. He said to Maggiore Verona, "Where in the world did you get this?"

"It's one of their propaganda leaflets."

"Obviously. But . . . well, do you mean they pass these out indiscriminately on the streets?"

"When we can't catch them, they do."

Horsten shook his massive head. "These people could use some lessons," he muttered. He went back to the propaganda leaflet, still registering disbelief. He shook his head in despair and, putting the pamphlet aside, turned to the Florentine.

"See here. We hardly know Citizen Juarez. However, as fellow strangers to Firenze and former shipmates on the *Half Moon*, I, at least, feel some duty toward him, to the extent that I feel bound to see he is adequately legally represented."

"Legally represented?" Verona said, puzzled. "But he's accused of being an Engelist."

Jerry poured another dollop of drink in his glass. He still stood at the room's bar. "Something missed me there. From what you said, all he's accused of is trying to get some books on Engelism. I might've done that myself, if I'd thought about it."

The maggiore said, "I would not advise it, Signore Rhodes. Perhaps it is true that your mother owns half the Catalina-Avalon planet complex, however, you are a long way from there, and here on Firenze we are very conscious of the subversives who wish to destroy our whole way of life."

Horsten said, "To get back to Zorro's legal representative. Ordinarily, undoubtedly he would have appealed to the United Planets Embassy, since it seems unlikely that Vacamundo would be represented diplomatically here. However, since the U.P. Embassy has been discontinued . . ."

"Undoubtedly, new representatives, uncontaminated by Engelist doctrine, will shortly be sent from Earth."

"Yeah, but meanwhile Zorro's in the jug," Helen said.

The Florentine looked at her.

Horsten said hurriedly, "Helen, you spend too much time looking at the Tri-Di historical crime shows."

"Look who's talkin'," Helen muttered. She went back to her box of toys.

Horsten said, "But what about Zorro's lawyer?"

"I told you," Maggiore Verona explained. "He's accused of being an Engelist. Obviously, no reputable attorney would represent him." He looked from Dorn Horsten to Jerry Rhodes, as nothing could be more obvious. "What would people think of a supposedly loyal Florentine who would represent an Engelist?"

"Not an Engelist," Jerry blurted. "Somebody *accused* of being an Engelist."

"Well," the other said stiffly. "You must admit, there's precious little difference. A mere technicality."

Jerry slugged down his drink. "I don't know," he said, a wild element in his voice. "I continually get the impression on this planet that everybody's kidding." He looked at the Florentine anti-subversion officer. "You sure you don't want a drink? Listen, something just occurred to me. You introduced yourself as attached to the Third Signore's staff. What did you say the Third Signore is in charge of?"

"Anti-subversion."

"What's that got to do with us? Why're you spending your time with us?"

The maggiore was a bit embarrassed, but still suave. "My dear Signore Rhodes. Surely it is the same on other worlds. Until evidence is presented to the contrary, we must operate on the, uh, possibility . . ." He let the sentence fade away.

Jerry grabbed up the bottle and poured himself another stiff one. "I'm beginning to think you people've been chasing these subversives so long you've gone drivel-happy." He gave the bottle a half wave in illustration. "You know what I ran into today at that sidewalk café? A guy who . . ."

Helen came up with a little plastic gun from her hatbox. She snarled at Jerry, pointing the gun, "Put down that bottle stranger. You had enough."

The maggiore laughed condescendingly. "Ah, little ragazza, you should never point a loaded weapon, unless you mean to use it."

Helen turned a beady eye on him. She swung the gun barrel in his direction. "Stick 'em up," she ordered. "You put my Uncle Zorro in the jug."

"Helen!" her father said in exasperation.

The Florentine was chuckling. He said in mock seriousness, "I refuse to stick 'em up. We loyal officers of the Third Signore never surrender."

"You asked for it," Helen said flatly and pulled the trigger.

"*Helen!*" her father blurted, rising from his chair in horror.

But the stream of water caught Maggiore Roberto Verona full in the face. He sat there frozen as it splattered over him. The water dribbled down over his lower face and onto his natty uniform.

Dr. Horsten was on his feet, a handkerchief in hand.

He dabbed at the besoaked Verona, roaring over his shoulder, "Helen! Go to your room! Immediately!"

Helen dropped the water pistol and, wailing, headed for the back rooms of the suite.

Maggiore Verona took a deep breath and collected himself with effort. He stood, holding up a hand to restrain the good doctor's efforts, and said shakily, "It is nothing. All apologies are accepted. She is but a little"—it took him an effort to bring out the last—"child."

He cleared his throat. "I must go. I must go change." He attempted a military bow, which didn't come off. "Signori, if you will excuse me." He headed for the door.

Dr. Horsten, continuing his chucking and incoherent apologies, saw him out, then returned to the oversized living room. There was storm in his expression.

"Where's that witch?"

Helen stuck her head through the double door that led back to the master bedroom, which she had taken over as her own domain.

"Coast clear?"

"What in the name of the . . ." Horsten began in wrath.

"Knock it," she muttered. She went over to the bar and ungraciously gave Jerry's leg a shove. She clambered up on a stool and reached for a bottle and glass.

"I had to shut him up some way," she said defensively. She gestured with her head at Jerry, a motion which made her little-girl curls flare out winningly. "He was about to blab about an *agent provocateur* we ran into, in town today."

Jerry, scowling, said, "What's an agent, whatever-you-said?"

"*Agent provocateur*," Helen repeated, gurgling liquid into her glass until Horsten turned his head away to avoid the sight. "Have you ever heard the old Czarist Russian saying? When four men sit down to talk revolution, three are police spies and the other a fool."

Jerry just looked at her.

"Well," she said. "Undoubtedly, that's our Great Marconi. Although I'm beginning to wonder."

"What are you talking about?" Horsten asked.

She told him about the Great Marconi and he scowled. He said, "What did you mean, you're beginning to wonder?"

Helen took a slug of her drink and sat down on the bar stool—she had been standing on it—and crossed her legs.

"Well, at first I figured he was secret police, trying to draw Jerry out, to see if he had any interest in Engelism."

81

"But now?"

She said thoughtfully, "Now I'm beginning to wonder if possibly he wasn't an Engelist pretending he was an Engelist."

"You threw that one too fast," Jerry protested.

Suddenly the front door of the penthouse suite opened and they turned to face it, all three frowning.

Zorro Juarez entered, his face as dark as when he had stormed out that morning.

He came up before them, his hands on his hips. "You know where I've just been?" he demanded.

"Yes," Helen said.

"That's what I thought. How'd you get me out?"

The three looked at him.

"We didn't," Jerry said. "If I got this straight, you weren't eligible to have a lawyer because you were accused of being an Engelist. How come you were silly enough to stick your neck out like that?"

"Look who's talking," Helen said, taking another slug of her drink. "You're hardly out of jail yourself."

Zorro was mystified. "Well, somebody evidently cut a lot of red tape, somehow. They had me in a sort of community cell, in a concentration camp. Everybody accused of subversion." He went over to the bar and without looking at the label of the bottle Helen had poured her drink from, upended it over a tall glass and let the golden, thickish beverage gush down.

"Engelists, eh?" Horsten nodded.

"No."

"No? What other kind of subversives are there on Firenze?"

Zorro took back a slug of his drink, looked down into the glass appreciatively, took another. "I wouldn't know. But my fellow jailbirds were the most unlikely candidates for membership in an underground organization you ever set eyes on."

Jerry said plaintively, "I don't know what there is about this evening. I don't seem to follow any of the conversation. Were these people Engelists, or not?"

The dark complected cowman growled, "If they were, they sure hid it from me. I tried to sound them out, individually and in groups. None of them knew anything about Engelism."

"Maybe they thought you were an *agent provocateur*," Jerry said, in newfound wisdom.

"What's that?"

Jerry looked at Helen from the side of his eyes. "A police spy stuck in with amateur revolutionists to draw them out."

Zorro thought about it. He shook his head finally. "No, that wasn't it. They weren't even particularly interested in the subject. Couldn't even get them to talk about it."

Horsten was scowling. "What did they talk about?"

"Mostly about the Dawnplanets."

VIII

IF HE HAD suddenly levitated to the ceiling, Zorro Juarez couldn't have set them further aback.

Zorro said, "I thought this alien intelligent life, the Dawnmen, were supposed to be a big United Planets secret."

Dorn Horsten, his face registering complete disbelief, made his way over to one of the room's overstuffed comfort chairs and sank down, dwarfing it.

"Supposedly they were," he said unhappily. "Helen and I didn't tell you the whole story. Neither of us were with Section G at the time, but we were briefed on the situation. It seems that when the Dawnworlds were first contacted, Ross Metaxa, along with the President of United Planets and the Director of the Commissariat of Interplanetary Affairs, brought together some two thousand of what they evidently thought were the most dependable chiefs of state of United Planets and laid the situation in their laps. I suppose they expected the conference to lead to greater cooperation among the member worlds."

"And . . ." Zorro prompted.

The scientist shrugged huge shoulders. "Evidently, the attempt proved successful with some. Metaxa tried to swear them all to secrecy. He should have known better. How can you swear two thousand highly individualistic men and women to secrecy?"

"They blabbed?"

"It would seem some of them did, from what you say. Otherwise, how would the man in the street, here on Firenze, know about even the existence of the Dawnworlds?"

Helen said in disgust, "Just how much were they aware of?"

Zorro made a gesture of discomfort. "Remember, I only spent a few hours in the place. But they knew that the aliens live on a small confederation of planets located some-

83

where out beyond Phrygia. And they'd got the rumor that the Dawnmen had fabulous discoveries that would make any human unbelievably rich and powerful if he could get his hands on them."

Horsten removed his glasses and ran a weary hand over his face. "Well," he said, "it's not our immediate problem. We're here to upset the Engelist applecart, and get Firenze back on the road to progress."

Zorro said, "Shouldn't we get in touch with Sid Jakes and let him know about this development?"

The big man shook his head. "They're too confoundedly conscious of all the paraphernalia involving communications, bugs, eavesdropping and such, here on Firenze. The police probably have every device known in U.P. to tap any signals we might send to Earth."

"Even a Section G communicator?" Jerry said. "I thought they were beyond tapping."

"There is no such thing as being beyond tapping," Horsten told him. "Our laboratories come up with something today, supposedly perfect, but in a year or so, or even a week or so, and some stute, somewhere, figures out a method of listening in. Whether or not the security people on Firenze have a way of cracking our communications with Earth, we don't know, but I don't think we ought to take any chances, particularly with nothing more important than this. Let's wait until we have something big, and we'll mention it, too, at the same time."

"It seems to me this is pretty big," Zorro said. "What's more important ultimately than the presence of the Dawn-worlds?"

"Ultimately, yes. But right now your assignment is to find out about these Firenze subversives and thwart them."

"So where do we start?" Helen said. She grunted disgust. "Thus far we know damn little more about them than we did when Metaxa briefed us back in the Octagon."

Jerry walked over to the vicinity of Dorn Horsten and sat down on the couch, his face in unwonted concentration. "You know," he said. "I still wonder if what we shouldn't do is go right to Roberto Verona and lay our cards on the table. If anybody knows anything about these Engelists, it's his Department of Anti-Subversion."

Helen grunted disgust again.

Zorro said, "I think we ought to get in touch with Sid Jakes and let him know about this Dawnworld development."

84

But Horsten was staring at Jerry. "You know," he said. "You're right."

"I am?"

Helen said, "Have you slipped around the corner? We open our traps to Verona about being interested in the Engelists and bingo, we're all in Zorro's concentration camp."

"Um," Horsten said, coming to his feet and looking at the chronometer on his wrist. "But we won't open our traps to Verona. What time is it getting to be? Late enough to burglarize a government office?"

"Oh, no," Helen protested.

"Oh, yes," Horsten said, beaming at her. "As Jerry says, if anybody knows anything about these Engelists, it's the Department of Anti-Subversion."

"Right," Jerry said, standing too. "With my luck, we'll stumble right on the guy who . . ."

"With your luck," Helen snorted, "we'll all break our legs, walking down stairs. Have you forgotten? That coin of yours isn't flipping heads any more."

"How do you mean?"

"Remember betting the waiter five to one?"

Jerry grinned. "That was lucky, wasn't it?"

"Lucky!" She glared at him.

"Sure. I was all set to pick up that Great Marconi fellow, the *agént provocateur*, and bring him back to the hotel. If I'd been able to get away with not paying that check, we'd all have been in the soup. As it was, they stuck me in jail, and the Great Marconi disappeared."

Helen deflated. "I never thought of that."

"Which reminds me," Jerry said to her. "You owe me a hundred interplanetary credits. Remember, you bet me that Zorro'd get killed in that duel."

"What!" Zorro yelped.

"Come on, let's get out of here," Helen said to Horsten. "I'd never be able to explain that."

It was getting dark when Helen and Horsten left the *Albergo Palazzo*, her hand in his as she tripped along, Gertrude and a little tin box *Dolly's Nurse Kit* in the other.

She said from the side of her mouth, her voice low enough that the casual passerby couldn't have heard, "Why didn't you want Jerry and Zorro? I hate to admit it, but Jerry's right. He's got the damnedest luck."

"That he has," Horsten said. "But sometimes it's a little too left-handed for my satisfaction. I'm continually waiting

85

for the roof to fall in and kill a fly that's been bothering friend Jerry."

"Well . . . Zorro, then."

"For this job," the big scientist said, "we need all the inconspicuous qualities we can muster. Zorro, cracking that overgrown whip of his, doesn't quite fit in."

"All right," Helen agreed. "So where is this Ministry of Anti-Subversion?"

"I wouldn't know," her companion said. "We'll have to ask."

"Ask?" Helen said bitterly. "And you talk about Zorro being conspicuous."

Dorn Horsten smiled fondly at her and chose that very moment to stop at the curbside where a uniformed Florentine was staring in despair at a small armored hovercar, embellished with the red letters, NATIONAL POLICE. The hood had been slid back to reveal the mechanism, but, on the face of it, the driver was stymied.

"What'm I ever going to tell the sergente," he muttered in suppressed rage. The scout car looked like nothing so much as a three-legged turtle, its tripod stilts supporting it some two feet off the surface of the street, in lieu of its now inoperative air cushion.

For the moment, the street was clear of other passersby. The scientist came to a halt, Helen still held by his hand, and said pleasantly, "Ah, my good fellow, could you give me a bit of direction?"

From the side of his mouth the police officer growled, "Dust off, Buster."

Horsten's eyebrows went up. "I merely wished to ask . . ."

The other turned and glowered at him. "Can't you see I'm busy? This damned tin can flicked out on me. Go on, dust." He turned back to contemplating his vehicle, muttering, "The sergente'll have my neck."

Horsten puffed out his cheeks.

"Take it easy, you big ox," Helen said lowly. "He's a cop."

Her companion ignored her. "I said I wished to ask some directions."

The furious minion of Firenze law spun on him, his teeth tight. "And I said to dust off. Can't you see I'm busy? I've got to cook up some explanation for my superior. He *told* me not to take this crate out. Anyway, dust. I haven't any time. . . ."

Horsten had started off the conversation with a benign - beam, that good-natured air attainable best by truly king-sized specimens of humanity. The beam was rapidly changing to a glare. "I shall give you exactly one more chance to tell me the location of the Ministry of Anti-Subversion," he said.

"Oh, you will, eh?"

"Yes."

"Come on, come on, Daddy!" Helen began to pull on her colleague's arm. Between her teeth she added, in a hiss, "Let's get out of here."

"Or you'll do just what?" the driver said.

Dorn Horsten looked at the armored police scout car. Its upper surface resembled the corrugated exterior of a hand grenade, or, perhaps, the shell of a turtle. The vehicle squatted there on its three sturdy metal stilts. It was a nasty looking little car.

Very deliberately, Horsten reached his hand out and banged the top of it with his closed fist. The three legs buckled, the end one to the point of allowing the rear of the armored scout to touch the street.

The driver looked at his vehicle for a long empty moment. Then he turned his eyes on the big scientist and looked at him. Finally, he looked down at Helen.

Helen wrinkled her nose at him nastily.

"You shoulda told my daddy," she said.

The policeman looked back at his car.

Finally he said to Horsten, "What was it you wanted to know?"

"Where is the Ministry of Anti-Subversion?"

"Over there." The other pointed. He looked back at the armored scout again, gloomily. "What'm I ever gonna tell the sergente?" he muttered.

Horsten hustled Helen across the street in the direction the police officer had indicated.

She looked at him bitterly. "Zorro's whip is too conspicuous," she said. "What'd you think is going to happen when that cop tells his sergeant what you just did? And why you did it. And where it was you wanted to go."

The algae specialist was all good nature again. He looked down at her. "If that man is stupid enough to tell his sergeant what happened, he'll undoubtedly wind up behind bars for drinking whilst on duty, my dear girl."

"I surrender," she muttered. "I give up."

They came to a halt and stared at the enormous building that confronted them.

"Ministry of Anti-Subversion," Horsten read with satisfaction.

"Closed," Helen said. "Look at the size of those bronze doors. The place looks like a cathedral."

"Um. However, someone should be here. Probably a night shift, or, at least, some guards."

"So we just knock?" Helen said hopefully, as he started off again, dragging her along.

"Well, I doubt if that would be effective. If they expected evening callers, undoubtedly there would be some entry provided, but all seems quite closed up."

"I can see it coming," Helen muttered glumly.

They stood before the gigantic bronze doors which dwarfed ten-fold even the oversized Dorn Horsten.

"There isn't even an identity screen, a method of summoning the nightman," Horsten said accusingly.

"All right, all right, you don't have to find excuses for me," Helen said. "I've been through the equivalent of this before." She looked back over her shoulder. There was a broad expanse of paved area before the building, and not a soul in sight. The vicinity of the Ministry of Anti-Subversion was evidently not sought out by the citizenry of Firenze, come the cool of evening.

Horsten took the large bronze doorknob in hand. It was an enormous, elaborate thing. He shook it. "Locked," he announced.

"Come on, come on," Helen said wearily.

He pulled, seemingly gently. He looked down at the knob, now in his hand. "It came out," he told her.

Helen grunted.

He put his huge paw against the door and shoved. Something inside the door groaned. He pushed a bit harder. Something rasped metallic complaint. Although his air seemed still one of gentle curiosity, his shoulders were now bunched.

"I'll be confounded," he said. "Open all the time."

"You damned mastodon," she said. "Come on. Inside, before somebody spots us."

They pushed their way in, the scientist closing the door behind. They looked about.

"Looks like Grand Central Station," Horsten muttered.

"What's that?" Helen said.

"Confound if I know. An idiomatic saying that comes down from antiquity; a connotation of being large in interior."

"Well, what do we do now?"

"I suppose we stroll about until we find someone."

"Oh, great. Or until somebody shoots us."

88

He looked down at her. "Now, who would shoot a nice little girl like you?"

She snorted at him. "Somebody who figures that nice little girls don't break into hush-hush government ministries."

Two massive stairways flanked a bank of a full dozen elevator shafts.

"Elevators," the big man said. "How anachronistic can you get? Have you noticed, my dear, they seem to go beyond the call of reason to maintain an air of yesteryear on this planet?"

Helen said, "Let's take the stairs. Then at least some stute won't be able to trap us between floors."

She caught onto his belt, gracefully bounded up to his shoulder, to save herself the climb. On the second floor, they looked up and down the extensive corridor that seemingly stretched away into infinity.

"All right," Helen said. "Do we keep climbing, or what? How do we find the department devoted to the Engelists? This place obviously doesn't run a night shift. And, for that matter, doesn't seem to boast much in the way of night . . ."

A voice behind them snapped, "Stand where you are!"

Dorn Horsten turned—and turned on his good-natured beam. "Ah, here we are," he said jovially. "I knew we'd find somebody!"

The other was a heavy-set, elaborately uniformed, suspicious looking officer who held a heavy scrambler in his right hand. He was about thirty feet from them and stood with his legs well parted and in a slight crouch: the stance of a fighting man.

He was not to be cozened. His heavy, somewhat brutal face bore several scars, mementoes of duel or street fights, or perhaps of military combat.

"Who are you?" he snapped.

Horsten jiggled little Helen on his shoulders to reassure her, and beamed at the other. "The question is, who are you, my dear fellow?"

Obviously the Florentine was confused by this confrontation, but was not to be put off his competent guard. "I'm Colonnello Fantonetti," he said, the weapon not wavering a particle. "Now, very quickly, who are you and what are you doing on the second floor of this ministry after closing hours?"

"I want down, Daddy!" Helen shrilled. "I'm afraid of that man."

89

Horsten said something and, ignoring the colonnello momentarily, slipped her to the floor, tucking Gertrude and the Dolly's Nurse Kit under his arm. Then he turned back to the Florentine.

"I came to inquire into the Engelists," he said, in a tone that might have been disarming had the words been other.

"The Engelists?" the armed man blurted. "You admit it?" Then, "How did you get in here?"

"I walked in," the big scientist said simply. He looked down at Helen, whose lower lip was trembling. "Now, now," he said. "After a time, Daddy will play allez-oop with you." He looked back at the anti-subversion officer. "So, you can tell me with whom I can get in touch in order to investigate thoroughly this Engelism program."

The other shook his head, as though unbelieving, but the gun didn't waver. He said, "This whole ministry is devoted to fighting the Engelists. I am head of my department. Luckily, I was working late tonight. You have explained nothing. You are under arrest." His eyes went to an empty desk which stood before the rank of elevator doors. On it was an orderbox and various switches and buttons. Still keeping his eyes on Dorn Horsten, as well as the muzzle of his scrambler, he started in that direction.

Helen said, "Allez-oop!"

The massive scientist had been holding her by one hand. Now, he suddenly flipped her upward, spun her, and flung her toward a stone column which stood some ten feet before the elevators.

The colonnello's trigger finger had, at the first motion, tightened, but then he stood there, eyes bugging.

In air, Helen seemed to become a ball then, at the last split moment, she turned, legs foremost, and struck the stone pillar. Seemingly, she bounced; somehow, upward. She seemed to spin in the air. A tiny human pinwheel, she turned and turned again. Hit the desk toward which the Florentine had been heading; caromed off in an impossible exhibition of tumbling; hit the metal door of one of the elevators, caromed off and struck immediately before the colonnello. She bounced high. His head reared back in alarm. She settled down, light as gauze, on his shoulder.

"Oooo," she said. "I musta slipped." Her right arm was around the startled officer's head, holding on tightly.

But her little left hand had a secure grip on the scrambler which, a moment ago, had been in his own supposedly competent grasp—and the muzzle was boring into his left ear.

Dorn Horsten was clucking as though in apology. "Now, dear," he scolded her, "do be careful. You might blow the colonnello's brains out." He frowned slightly, as though in inner debate. "Assuming . . ." he added, but let the sentence dribble away.

The Florentine was frozen.

Horsten approached and took the gun from Helen's hand and she dropped gracefully to the floor and smoothed out her pretty blue dress in an exaggerated little-girl gesture.

The scientist said, and there was authority in his voice now, "Where's your office?"

Still dazed, the other indicated. "In there."

"All right, let's all go in there."

Herding the colonnello before them, Horsten and his diminutive companion entered the office. It was large but standard, with the usual conglomeration of desks, files and office equipment, including orderboxes and voco-typers.

Even as Helen, humming under her breath, put her Dolly's Nurse Kit on the larger desk and began pulling play vials and hypo needles forth, the big scientist ushered the captive to a chair.

The self-named Colonnello Fantonetti was not a coward. He grated, "What do you want? I warn you . . ."

Horsten silenced him with a wave of the pistol. "Just as I told you, information about the Engelists."

"You're obviously Engelists yourselves," the other rasped.

"To the contrary, my dear fellow."

It turned out that Helen's play hypodermic needles were not exactly toys. She efficiently swabbed a section immediately above his wrist—not taking the time to have him remove his tunic, and roll up a sleeve—and pressed home a shot. She then returned her Dolly's Nurse equipment to its box and bounded up into a chair very neatly.

Horsten said to the victim, "Scop, you know. Sorry it's necessary. But we're quite keen about finding out all there is to know on the Engelists."

The other gritted his teeth. "You can't escape," he said, somewhat out of context with the subject.

"Um," Horsten said. He looked down at his wrist chronometer and made impatient tush, tush noises while he waited. Helen sat there quietly, smiling in childlike innocence at the colonnello until that worthy, in disgust, closed his eyes to escape.

Horsten said finally, "What is your name?"

The colonnello had blisters of cold sweat on his forehead and he tried desperately to hold his lips tight. However, finally they opened.

"Salvador Marie Fantonetti."

"And your position?"

"Colonnello, on the staff of His Eccellenza, Alberto Scialanga, the Third Signore."

"What are your duties?"

"To combat the Engelists."

"Who are the Engelists?"

"Subversives who wish to overthrow the government of the First Signore and the Free Democratic Commonwealth of Firenze."

Dorn Horsten said, "How do they expect to accomplish this?"

There was a slight hesitation in the drugged man's voice. Finally, "I do not know."

Horsten scowled. "Well, what methods do they use?"

"They attempt to subvert the institutions of Firenze."

"Of course, but how?"

"By . . . by speaking against the First Signore and his Council of Signori."

Helen said, "Do they have radio, Tri-Di, other broadcasting facilities?"

"No."

"Well, do they have newspapers?" She was scowling in growing puzzlement as was her partner.

The colonnello remained silent.

She reworded it. "Do you think they have newspapers?"

"No."

Dorn Horsten said impatiently, "Do they write books against the government?"

The Florentine remained silent.

"Do you think they write books against the government?"

"I . . . I do not know."

"Do you know of any pamphlets, leaflets or other printed propaganda they have written against the government?"

"No."

Helen said, a touch of disbelief in her voice, "What do they do in their attempts to overthrow the government?"

"They attempt to recruit followers to their underground by speaking against the administration of the First Signore."

Helen and Dorn Horsten looked at each other.

The scientist started on a new tack. "Have you ever captured any Engelists?"

Their prisoner of the Scop drug remained silent.

Frowning his growing bewilderment, Horsten demanded,

92

"Have you ever captured any persons you suspected of being Engelists?"

"Yes."

"How many of these did you prove were Engelists?"

He remained silent.

"Did you prove any of them were Engelists?" Helen said impatiently.

"No."

The two stared at him.

Finally Helen snapped, "Have you ever, in your whole career, seen a person that you absolutely knew was an Engelist?"

The hesitation was there once more. Finally, "No."

Now they really goggled him. Helen snapped, "Look. How do you know there are any Engelists?"

"They attempt to subvert the institutions of the Free Democracy of the Commonwealth of Firenze."

"That's not what I asked you," she snarled. She looked up at Horsten. "What in the hell's going on?"

He was tugging on the lobe of his right ear and staring at their victim. "You know . . ." he said.

"What?"

"I think this man's been memory-washed or something."

"Are you zany? He's a colonel in their damned Anti-Subversion Ministry. Who'd memory-wash him?"

"How would I know?" he said impatiently.

She jumped to the floor, went back to the desk where her Dolly's Nurse Kit sat.

"What're you doing?"

"What do you think I'm doing? Giving him a shot of our own memory-wash. What else is there to do? He doesn't know a thing about the Engelists."

Horsten, followed by Helen, pushed his way through the door of the penthouse suite and strode on into the living room. He came up abruptly.

"What in the name of Holy Jumping Zen are you doing?" he roared.

Zorro Juarez and Jerry Rhodes looked up. Helen's hatbox of toys sat next to them on the floor. Zorro was cross-legged before a cocktail table. Jerry stood next to him. On the table was propped one of Helen's gadget toys, a supposed miniature Tri-Di set. Even at this distance, Horsten and Helen could make out a face on the screen of the device.

Zorro said, "Making a report to Sid Jakes."

93

The two newcomers to the scene approached nearer, until the face of the Section G assistant head was clear to their view too.

Jakes grinned at them. "How goes the assignment?"

"It doesn't," Horsten growled, after shooting a disapproving glance at his two associates. "We just broke into one of the Firenze ministries devoted to local subversive activities. We put a mucky-muck we found there under Scop."

"Neat trick." Sid Jakes grinned. "Why? And what did you find out?"

"Not a damn thing," Helen snorted. "This is the most underground underground in the history of undergrounds."

Dorn Horsten looked down into the small screen of the communicator. "So far, we've drawn a blank. I assume Zorro's told you that evidently the Engelists got to the files of agent Bulchand before we were able to discover what, if anything, he had on them."

"Yes." Sid Jakes nodded, over the light-years. His usually exuberant voice clouded slightly. "He also told me that everybody and his cousin on Firenze seems familiar with the Dawnworld story."

Horsten shot another look at Zorro, whose face was registering a certain amount of defiance. The scientist said, "I wasn't in favor of making this report at this time. Evidently Zorro and Jerry have overridden my opinion."

Sid Jakes pursed his lips. "I doubt if there's any connection, but we've had a complication here on the same matter. I might as well mention it, on the off chance that that you'll turn up something there on Firenze. Be a neat trick if you do. I can't see any reason to believe . . ." He let it fade off.

All four of his subordinates were frowning at him.

Sid Jakes grinned. "Ronny Bronston is still in the hospital, but his office was broken into early this morning."

"Broken into?" Helen said. "Right there in the Octagon?"

He didn't answer her directly. His grin turned rueful. "Somebody stole the starchart."

Jerry said, "The starchart giving the location of the Dawnworlds?"

Sid Jakes looked at him, his head cocked slightly. "How did you know?"

But at that moment a voice from the entryway boomed, "His Zelenza, the First Signore of the Free Democratic Commonwealth of Firenze!"

"Oh, oh," Sid Jakes said, in the tiny screen, "you people have times there, don't you? Let me know later. Off." His grinning face faded.

But the four were already staring at the entry.

There were two ultra-efficient looking guards with unfamiliar type of handweapons at the ready, flanking the door. Their eyes were straight ahead, their expressions those of the goon down through the centuries.

He of the booming voice stood between them. Though in mufti, he was obviously to uniform born. His eyes swept them, swept the room in quick check. He stepped back, a double step, and faced the door, as though deity were about to enter.

Maggiore Roberto Verona and one other came through it. Whoever the other was, he obviously outranked the maggiore. His uniform was magnificent and well bespattered with decorations.

Helen had adjusted well enough to say sotto voce to Jerry, "The fewer the wars, the more medals the big brass wear." She had scooped up the disguised communicator and placed in it Gertrude's toy hands.

The man who was obviously none other than the First Signore came striding in, quite obviously at his full ease.

"Apologies everyone, apologies," he called, his voice casual. "Maggiore, I believe you are acquainted with our friends from overspace. The honors, please."

The First Signore was a man barely in his mid-thirties but bore the air of command as though it had been with him since the cradle. But his, also, was the ages-old face of the politician; the open friendliness, the so-evident sincerity, the obvious integrity, the love of his fellow man.

"Already, I don't like this guy," Helen muttered.

"Shh," Horsten hissed.

Maggiore Verona said, his voice indicating the degree to which he was overwhelmed by being in the presence of his ultimate chief, "Your Zelenza, may I present the celebrated Dr. Dorn Horsten, and the Signorina Helen Horsten?"

"An honor, Your Zelenza," the doctor said, bowing to the

exact extent a noted scientist would be expected to, to a chief of state of a member world of U.P.

Helen stared, put her thumb in her mouth, caught herself, pulled it out and stuck both her hands behind her back, and continued to stare, her little feet toe-ing in.

"The honor is mine, Doctor. I am informed your work is known from one extent of the confederation to the other." The First Signore bowed. And to Helen, "My, what a pretty dolly you have there."

"His Eccellenza Gerald Rhodes, entrepreneur from the planet Catalina."

Jerry said, projecting the fact that in his time he had met many a bigwig, "A pleasure, Your Zelenza."

The First Signore eyed him appraisingly. "My pleasure, Signore Rhodes. I am told you visit our world with the possible intention of taking advantage of its many opportunities."

Maggiore Verona continued, the heartiness in his voice fading somewhat. "His Eccellenza, Zorro Juarez, of the planet Vacamundo."

The chief executive of Firenze said, "Ah yes, Signore. I understand that you have already had an unfortunate experience with our necessarily stringent regulations against dissident elements."

Zorro said defensively, "I was simply trying to find out something about these Engelists everybody talks about."

"Of course. Unfortunately you went about it in the wrong manner. One of my council heard of the matter and took care of it. I, personally, shall be happy to give you any information you may require, when opportunity permits."

His eyes swept the four of them in hospitality, and he strode toward the bar, saying over his shoulder, "Maggiore, please explain the situation." He took up a glass and let his eye run over the collection of bottles.

Maggiore Verona had followed him into the living room proper, leaving the other newcomers still in the entrada.

"Dr. Horsten, Signori," he said. "There has been a change in the plans of His Zelenza. He has decided, after all, personally to attend the pseudo-election."

Helen looked at Jerry from the side of her eyes and murmured softly, "Ha. The Rhodes luck. Tossed out on the street."

"However," the anti-subversion officer hastened to add, "His Zelenza insists that all efforts be made to secure other quarters for you."

His Zelenza, not bothering to listen, was holding up to the light the bottle which Zorro and especially Helen had been drawing upon for refreshment. In his left hand was a tiny glass, on his face an expression of shock. He said, "My Betelgeuse Chartreuse!"

Horsten was exploring the situation with the unhappy Roberto Verona, assisted by Zorro Juarez. However, Jerry Rhodes was of more practical stuff. He approached the ultimate head of the Firenze state, nonchalantly flipping his French franc.

He cleared his throat. "Ah, Your Zelenza."

"Yes, Signore?"

"It occurs to me that there are seven bedrooms in all in this suite."

"Oh?" The other frowned. "I don't believe I've ever counted. Seven, eh?"

"Seven," Jerry said definitely. He flipped the coin, caught it. "It occurs to me that possibly you are a man not unaccustomed to taking a chance now and then."

"A chance?"

"A bit of a gamble."

The First Signore tore his eyes from his bottle. "You have touched on my weakness, Signore. But I am not sure I follow."

Jerry flipped the coin again. "I am willing to wager a flat hundred thousand interplanetary credits against my being allowed to remain in my room, here in the suite, that I can call the flip of this coin."

"A . . . hundred . . . *thousand* . . . interplanetary . . . credits!"

Jerry flipped the coin, caught it, flipped again, a great nonchalance in his air.

This time it was the First Signore who cleared his throat. "I'll flip the coin," he said flatly. "You call it."

"Right." The coin changed hands.

His Zelenza looked at both sides. "This is heads, this is tails, eh? Very well." He flipped it, caught it, slapped it down on the back of his left hand, covered it with his right.

Jerry said, "Heads".

The other peered, scowled, shook his head. "You win."

Jerry put his hands in his pockets. "Same bet," he said. "This time for the right of Dr. Horsten and his daughter to remain in their rooms."

"I say, you are a sportsman."

"One hundred thousand interplanetary credits." Jerry nodded.

"You're on," the First Signore said. He flipped, caught the coin again, peered at it suspiciously.

"Tails, this time," Jerry said.

The scowl deepened. "You've won again."

"And now . . ." Jerry began.

"Your Zelenza!" Roberto Verona blurted.

His Zelenza was scowling unhappily at the coin.

The maggiore said quickly to Zorro, "Unfortunately, the First Signore's staff is such that additional room simply can't be spared. Happily, there is, down in the basement, an emergency room vacated by an assistant janitor. . . ."

"Oh, no," Zorro protested.

The Firenze chief of state returned the coin, albeit reluctantly. He said to Jerry Rhodes, "Given time, I must introduce you to my own favorite game, poker."

The two goons with their highly bemedaled superior had departed the entrada and now marched through the living room on what was obviously a security tour of inspection of the suite.

His Zelenza returned to his bottle, and drop by drop poured the thick golden liquid into his tiny liqueur glass. He half filled it, then carefully put it down. He returned the crystal stopper to the bottle, opened a small door set below in the bar, inserted the bottle on a shelf, closed the door, locked it with a small golden key, which he stashed away in a pocket of his jerkin. Muttering, he took the glass made made his way toward the living room's throne-like, most comfortable chair—formerly, the usual domain of Helen.

To one side, the maggiore was explaining to an indignant Zorro. To the rear of the penthouse suite, the bodyguards were making their room-to-room check. Dorn Horsten stood in owl-like magnificence, every inch the stolid, absent-minded scientist. Jerry, his accommodations taken care of, had sunk oafishly onto a couch.

His Zelenza began to lower himself into his comfort chair, a sigh of anticipated relaxation already on his lips.

"Hey," Helen squeaked.

He caught himself in suspension, stuck there; turned to inspect his destination. There was approximately thirty-five pounds of femininity that hadn't been there a moment ago immediately below his derrière. In his attempt to avert disaster, he jerked, spilling a portion of the contents of his carefully cherished glass.

His Zelenza came erect.

A score of feet away, Maggiore Verona, who had caught the action, froze, his shoulders hunched up as though in defense against dangerous developments.

However, a malady-laden smile struggled for existence on the First Signore's face. He took an audible breath, then, in ultimate sacrifice, took his place on the same great couch occupied by Jerry Rhodes.

Helen, at her ease, crossed her plump legs and said, conversationally, "Whatcher name?"

His Zelenza blinked, looked around for minions to come to his support, found none. He refrained from his drink, and said, "I beg your pardon, little Principessa?"

Helen said confidentially, "Whatcher real name?"

The chief of state of Firenze let his eyes go from right to left, covering the vicinity. For the moment, there seemed none witnessing the conversation; Dorn Horsten was involved in a low talk with Jerry about moving their luggage to rooms which would conflict least with the First Signore's staff; Maggiore Verona was still in verbal combat with the miffed Zorro.

His Zelenza said condescendingly, "You mean, what does my mama call me?"

Helen looked at him in childlike flatness. She shook her head. "I don't care what your old lady calls you. Whatcher name?"

Horsten, evidently not as absorbed in his conversation as all that, turned, and called, "Helen!"

Helen was wide-eyed innocence. "All I said was whatzis name. I can't call him Uncle Hizelenza, if he's gonna live with us." All of a sudden she began to pucker up. "He's gonna move into my *big* room," she wailed.

The massive scientist came over hurriedly. "Now, see here . . ." he began.

"I *like* my big room. And so does Gertrude," Helen wailed.

"Who is Gertrude?" The First Signore said to nobody in particular, and was ignored, probably for the first time in his memory.

The suite was being invaded by additional uniformed, faceless Florentines, some bearing personal luggage of their ultimate superior, some of his immediate staff, complete with briefcase and office equipment, all carrying the air of competence inevitable in those connected with supreme authority. Zorro's luggage passed in the opposite direction, in the hands of two of the goons, a deflated Zorro following.

The maggiore came up hurriedly. "Doctor," he said in despair, "His Zelenza has been most gracious. . . ."

The First Signore was evidently reaching some sort of an edge under the impetus of Helen's keening. He had come to his feet again, his glass, containing what was evidently his idea of the ultima thule of potables, temporarily abandoned on a cocktail table.

He said, between his teeth, "Not at all, Maggiore. The little Principessa is our guest. How charming that her father allowed her the master bedroom. She shall retain it. Who is Gertrude, a nurse?"

"A nurse?" Helen said, immediately turning off the temperament, in view of victory. "Gertrude's a boy. Gertrude's an Engelist."

"An Engelist!" the First Signore uttered. By this time, his face had surrendered its air of supreme command of the local situation; in fact, there was an element of being lost in bedlam.

The maggiore said hurriedly, "Gertrude is her doll, Your Zelenza. The little girl has heard others speaking of the subversives since her arrival. She . . . she doesn't understand."

"Ha!" Helen said darkly.

Two aides approached, each, evidently, with messages for their chief.

At long last, he had someone at whom to roar.

He roared.

The aides disappeared magically.

The First Signore, now well shaken, turned to the liqueur glass of his treasured Golden Chartreuse. He took it up, began its journey to his lips, came to a bewildered halt, stared unbelievingly into the empty crystal. His expression clearly reflected that he couldn't remember finishing the drink and that he couldn't quite believe that he had. For the briefest of moments he looked at Helen, who stood nearest the short table upon which the glass had rested, but then he shook his head in inner disbelief.

He turned and made his way to the bar. It took him a moment to recall that he had put the bottle under lock. He fumbled for the tiny golden key, finally located it and acquired the bottle. He made an initial motion toward refilling the small liqueur glass, but then, shaking his head again, put it to one side and reached for a tumbler.

Maggiore Roberto Verona was staring at his superior; on the face of it, he had never seen the First Signore in

100

this condition. He shook his head and turned back to his duties.

The hustle and bustle was beginning to subside somewhat, the efficiency of the underlings not being affected by the contretemps to which their chief was being subjected.

Jerry Rhodes, who had gone through this slumped on his couch, hands in pockets, said to his host, "What's a pseudo-election?"

The First Signore had regained control. He made his way back to his recently evacuated position, tumbler firm in his grasp. He suddenly became aware of the fact that in the background not only Maggiore Verona, but several others of his staff were eyeing him in untoward wise.

He snapped, "Out. Everybody, out. I suddenly find myself weary."

"Undoubtedly, the trip down . . ." the maggiore began smoothly.

"Whatever," the First Signore snapped. "Out! I . . . I wish to have a relaxed few moments with my new . . . uh, friends from overspace. Anything for a . . ." He cut himself off in mid-sentence and finished with simply, "Everybody out!"

They scooted.

The chief executive of Firenze sank back against the couch cushions and closed his eyes. He muttered, loud enough to be heard, "I must be getting old," but then, he cleared his throat, popped his eyes open, sat more erect and brought himself under control.

"That is—what was the question?"

"Whatcher real name?" Helen said.

For the briefest of moments, it seemed as though he was going to close his eyes again, but he straightened. He looked at her, attempting the patronizing air of the adult toward the eight-year-old. It didn't quite come off.

"Antonio Cesare Bartolemo d'Arrezzo . . . little Principessa."

Helen thought about it. "That's too long," she announced.

Antonio Cesare Bartolemo d'Arrezzo smiled benignly at her and turned to Jerry. "You asked about the election?"

Dorn Horsten by now had also settled to rest. He said, "I was interested too, though politics are far from my forte. You called it a pseudo-election?"

"The term, then, isn't universal throughout United Planets?"

"Not exactly," Horsten said

Jerry Rhodes had come to his feet and gone over to the bar. He reached for a glass and then . . .

The First Signore restrained himself, though the torment of unrequited hope washed his face. All in vain. He had forgotten to return his treasured bottle to its locked chamber. The glass Jerry had selected was of highball capacity. He returned with it half full to his seat.

He managed to turn on a condescending beam. "Pseudo-election," he said. "But surely the institution is well-founded in the traditions of antiquity."

They looked at him. Even Helen.

The First Signore, on his own grounds now, was expansive. "I suppose the institution took real form in the Twentieth Century, back on Mother Earth, though it was not unknown earlier. Ah, the Third Reich is as good an example as any. If your history serves you, you'll recall that Adolf was unsuccessful in winning a majority in the crucial elections, somewhat to the surprise of industrial monopolists, such as Thyssen and Krupp, who were backing him. It was necessary to have President Hindenberg, supposedly of the opposition, appoint him chancellor. Shortly after, Adolf thoughtfully eliminated all other political organizations and in the future polled some ninety-five percent of the vote. An even better example, perhaps, was to be found in the, uh, Republic of Russia."

"You mean the Union of Soviet Socialist Republics?" Horsten said, intrigued now.

The First Signore smiled encouragingly. "Exactly. Wonderful name, eh? Shows vivid imagination. Here, the leaders of the Dictatorship of the Proletariat—who the proletariat was dictating to is somewhat obscure, since supposedly all other classes had been liquidated—had long since decided that one party was sufficient, and eliminated unnecessary confusion on the part of the electorate, hence garnering a comfortable majority of some ninety-seven percent, give or take a point or two in each election to betoken authenticity."

"So"—Jerry nodded—"you carry on in the tradition of the Nazis and communists."

"Oh, no, no," the First Signore protested. He took up his glass momentarily for his long postponed sip, but put it down again in the enthusiasm for his subject. "Firenze is in the tradition of the great democracies, such as Great Britain and the States, to continue to draw example from the same era. In such case, their political party often achieved even better than ninety-seven percent of the vote."

His audience of three blinked in unison.

Horsten said apologetically, "I labored under the impression that in those countries they had more than one party."

"No, no. Optical illusion, camouflage, double-take—or whatever it was they called it in those days. In England they had the Conservative Labor Party and in the States the Republican Democrats, though in both cases there was the optical illusion of two parties. In actuality, they stood for the same thing, the status quo, represented the same elements and couldn't be told apart. The electorate, admittedly, was given the, uh, fun of turning one wing of the party out, periodically, and replacing it with the other, but it made no difference. Oh, don't misunderstand. Other candidates appeared from time to time, though largely, election laws were such that minority parties were as banned as they were in the Reich. Such protest opposition votes as did get through, when they were counted at all, were largely write-in candidates. Two, Pogo and Donald Duck, were among the more popular—two political figures of whom little comes down to us. Others sometimes made a brief play for the write-in vote. Twiggy and Batman come to my mind; once again, their principles, platforms and so forth, have been lost to us in the ages. But Donald Duck and Pogo were contestants for several elections running. Someone like the perennial Norman Thomas, whom I sometimes suspect of having been desirous of joining his organization to that of the Republican Democrats, making it the Republican Democrat Socialist Party. He once complained that Roosevelt had taken over his whole platform."

"I'm not really that far up on political history," Horsten said, impressed by the other's erudition. "I am surprised that you are."

The First Signore shrugged in modesty. "Of course, we of the families who are particularly interested in politics begin our training quite early in life." He reached for his glass again. Looked at it in some surprise. Frowned. Scowled. Thought about it some more. Squinted at the liquid level still once again, gave up and took a sip. When he put the glass down this time, it remained a bit nearer to him than before.

"So this pseudo-election you hold . . ." the scientist prodded.

"Is in the best of democratic traditions," the First Signore said.

"But it's not a *real* election?" Jerry said.

"Of course it is a real election. Every five years we
103

hold one. It's a national holiday. Very popular. Everyone eligible must vote. There are penalties if one doesn't. It's done very properly. Secret ballot, and all. We pretend we have no record of those who vote for Pogo or . . ."

"Pogo!" Helen blurted.

There was a mystified element on the face of the chief of state of Firenze. "Surprisingly enough, the name of this candidate has come down through the centuries, evidently as a symbol of protest. Since our citizenry is compelled to vote, some resort to writing in the mysterious historical personage, rather than vote for the party candidate."

"Party candidate?" Horsten echoed, in way of prompting.

"Yes, of course. In the far past, on Firenze, we had four political parties which originally stood for differing principles. However, as this sometimes proved disconcerting for the responsible elements in our socioeconomic scheme of things, they coalesced until we had the Holy Temple Radicals and the Liberal Conservatives."

There was confusion in the eyes of Jerry Rhodes. "But *now* . . ." he said, as though with hope.

"Well, now, in the face of the threat of the Engelists, the two have joined into the Machiavellian Party."

"Machiavellian Party?" Helen bleated, before she could remember to keep in character.

The First Signore beamed at her. "Yes, little Principessa." He chuckled ruefully. "I am afraid the full significance of the name of this great statesman of the past is lost to us, but he was once most prominent in the original Firenze, or Florence, as it was called in Amer-English, and later Earth Basic."

Helen muttered something to Gertrude.

Jerry said quickly, covering Helen's break, "And how large a percentage of the vote do the Engelists rack up?"

The other stared at him, as though the visitor from overspace was jesting in very bad taste.

"Do you think us ridiculous enough to allow those subversives on the ballot?"

"Oh. Oh, of course not," Jerry said soothingly. "Obviously not. A pseudo-election. Nobody but the Machiavellian Party. Secret ballot. If anybody casts a write-in for Pogo or some other protest vote, you don't let them know you've kept a record of it."

"Correct," the First Signore said, happy that all was understood. "As the Seventh Signore, of the Firenze Bureau of Investigation, once pointed out, that man who will cast a vote for Pogo today, is a potential subversive tomorrow."

Horsten got back into the scene. "Your Zelenza, you must excuse our ignorance. There are so many socioeconomic systems, so many political forms, in United Planets, that it is most difficult to keep universally informed. If I understand correctly, the Firenze chief executive is entitled the First Signore, and is assisted by a cabinet of nine?"

"Quite correct. The Second Signore is our Chief of Security; the Third Signore, Maggiore Verona's superior, heads the Ministry of Anti-Subversion; the Fourth Signore is in charge of Counter-Espionage; the Fifth, the AFA, short for Anti-Firenze Activities; the Sixth Signore has control of Central Intelligence; the Seventh is Director of the Bureau of Investigation; the Eighth, Commissioner of the National Police; the Ninth Signore heads the Department of Internal War; and the Tenth Signore holds the portfolios of State, Interior, Justice, Revenue, Agriculture, Trade, Health and Education."

There was a silence on the part of the newcomers from overspace. The First Signore took the opportunity to reach for his glass again.

"Tony?" Helen said, twisting her rose-red little mouth in childish thoughtfulness.

"Eh?" The First Signore of the Free Democracy of the Commonwealth of Firenze was obviously taken aback by her form of address.

"Your name's too long."

Jerry said, in a hurry, "That Tenth Signore. He's kind of low man on the totem pole, eh?"

The Florentine nodded to acknowledge the question. "Ah, perhaps, but believe me, Michael is just as necessary"—he shook his finger here at Jerry, in way of emphasis —"to free government as any of the rest of this administration. I wish to assure you, Signore Rhodes, that all is tranquil here on Firenze. Your investments and those of your colleagues on Catalina would be safe. Ah, which reminds me. In what form do you have this variable capital you are considering investing in our many opportunities?" As though absently, he came to his feet, went over to the bar and put his precious bottle back under lock and key.

Jerry was off-hand. "What form? Oh, naturally, the most negotiable."

The First Signore continued to look at him expectantly.

Jerry said, "Mother was anxious to be liquid, in case an immediate opportunity or so was available."

"Oh, believe me, there are many. But in what form is

105

your capital?" The First Signore chuckled. "Obviously, not in Firenze currency, which, after all, is the most negotiable exchange possible—on Firenze."

Jerry's eyes were going blank, but his luck held and he was taken off the hook by the front door banging open. The highly uniformed security officer, who had earlier supervised the First Signore's arrival, came through. Immediately behind was a cluster of others in some agitation.

"What is the meaning of this!" d'Arrezzo snapped. "I ordered that I not be disturbed." He strode several steps forward.

Helen gave a sigh of relief, snaked out a hand and snagged the glass of priceless potable, and took a quick snort. She shot a look of disgust at the hapless Jerry even as she quickly returned the glass under the glare of Dorn Horsten.

"Geneva," she muttered to Jerry. "Your money would be on Geneva."

Half a dozen newcomers were in the entrada.

"Your Zelenza!" the officer commanding said apologetically. "We have just captured this Signore, attempting to enter your presence! In view of his identity . . ."

Helen said, "Why, it's the Great Marconi!"

X

THE NEWCOMER winced but shaking loose the two security men who hung onto his arms, honored Helen with a bow. "The Great Marconi, Signorina." He came forward. His eyes, as ever, overly bright, swept the others in the living room, winding up with the First Signore, whose face was less than welcoming.

There was a quirk of amusement in the Great Marconi's expression. He sweepingly bowed once again. "Ah, Cousin Antonio, you will forgive me if I forego the traditional affectionate embrace. A touch of the steel in my most re-. cent affair, you know. The arm is a bit stiff."

The First Signore said, "Cesare, you are well acquainted with our arrangement." He turned back to the security men. "Leave us!"

The officer hesitated. The Florentine chief of state looked at him.

"Yes, Your Zelenza." He turned and the guard contingent bustled out with him.

The First Signore returned to the newcomer, who grinned mockingly. "My dear Antonio, no matter your lofty rank—

106

as of the moment—and my lowly position in the scheme of things, I cannot guarantee complete lack of contact, particularly if you insist on leaving your official estates and coming here to our somewhat grimy capital."

"I am not speaking, obviously, of chance encounter. But your presence can only embarrass me, in view of my office. Your sworn agreement was not to seek out . . ."

The Great Marconi spread his hands in a most Latin gesture, the palms up, his eyebrows up as well. "My dear Antonio, I had no idea you were here. The Tri-Di news broadcasts had it that you would conduct your campaign on the air and from the, uh, safety of the palace."

"Safety!" the other blurted, his expression going suddenly empty. "Are you impugning my courage, Cesare, by . . ." In mid-sentence, he broke it off. He said, frowning, "But if you were not seeking me . . ."

Cesare Marconi smiled broadly. "You are much too vain, Cousin Antonio. I have other friends than those numbered in the ranks of my relatives." He turned to Jerry, who had been taking this in, in fascination. "How unfortunate that we became separated at the café, my dear, uh, Cross Rhodes."

Jerry snorted.

The newcomer said cheerily, "I have come to discuss with you the matters in which you expressed interest."

Helen said, "Oh, oh," and darted a look at the Florentine chief executive.

Dorn Horsten stepped forward. "Uh . . ." he began.

But the First Signore waved a hand negatively and in disgust. "Undoubtedly, my Cousin Cesare informed your young friend that he was an Engelist. He knows about as much of Engelism as I do of the archaeology of the Denebian planets."

His seedily appareled cousin, even as he made his way toward the bar, said with cheer, "If you were not immune, through your lofty position, Antonio, I would call you out." He turned his back to them and inspected critically the collection of potables.

"Any time . . ." the First Signore began heatedly.

Cesare Marconi half turned and the easy-going mask stripped away. "Yes? You were about to say?"

His cousin switched gears, though obviously in inner heat. "I was about to say that your Engelism is a pose, to embarrass me. You actually know nothing about the subversive movement, which is exactly why you are tolerated in your making a spectacle of yourself and your family."

Cesare Marconi had returned to his perusal of the beverages. "Um," he murmured. "Where's the Chartreuse? Hidden again? Antonio, you were a tight money pincher as a boy and being on the ultimate expense account hasn't changed you." He took up a bottle and scowled at the label. "What's whiskey?"

"It's from Earth," Dorn Horsten said. "Distilled from cereal. Alcohol is the sole depressant involved."

"I'll try it." Marconi nodded, pouring a tumbler half full.

"Usually," Horsten said, "you mix a small amount with something."

"Oh? Doesn't that diffuse the flavor?"

"Yes."

The Great Marconi took a sip, flinched, but refused to retreat before strangers. He returned with the glass to a chair, seated himself and crossed his legs.

"You are quite incorrect," he told the First Signore. "I am thoroughly acquainted with Engelism, its origins, the conditions which brought it about, even its goals. However, mine is, you might say, a wing of the movement. A splinter element which has split away. The Engelists, we are told, desire to overthrow the present socioeconomic system by force and violence. Of this, my wing disapproves, seeking the basic change necessary by peaceful means, by civilized use of the ballot. Which is, of course, not against the Constitution of the Free Democracy of the Commonwealth of Firenze."

His cousin was fuming. "As you are aware, the Constitution is temporarily being held in abeyance during the emergency. Until the subversives have been brought under control, civil rights and some of our political guarantees must be sacrificed." He turned to Dorn Horsten. "He speaks gibberish. His so-called wing of the Engelists which wishes to overthrow the government by vote isn't even on the ballot."

"No fault of mine," Marconi said, trying another sip of the drink. He made a face. "This stuff is worse than grappa." Then, "You keep everybody off the ballot but yourselves. However, in the long run it will do you no good. You can't change the weather by fiddling with the thermometer, and you can't prevent a revolution by miscounting, or not counting at all, the votes of the majority."

"You think the Engelists a majority?" The other laughed.

"Not yet, not yet, but they will be."

108

There was a gentle hum from some unknown source and the perturbed Florentine chief snapped, "Yes!"

Into the entrada came one of the highly uniformed members of the staff who had been about earlier. He said, "Your Zelenza, the meeting of the Council."

"Eh? Oh, yes, of course." The First Signore looked from his cousin to the otherworlders and back again, evidently came to a decision and snapped to Horsten, "He is the family . . . jester. You might keep it in mind." Without further farewell, he marched to the entrada and the front door, which opened before him.

Helen looked at Cesare Marconi. "Tony thinks you're a phony-baloney, Mr. The Great Marconi."

"The feeling has long been reciprocated, Signorina," the Florentine told her. He came to his feet again and made his way to the bar and scowled down at it. "He's probably got it locked up," he muttered.

The massive scientist came over to Helen and squint-eyed down at her. "Are you drenched?" he said accusingly.

"On that lilac-water?" She snorted.

The door through which the First Signore had just left had not closed behind him. Through it now, came Zorro Juarez, a harassed air upon him. Maggiore Verona brought up the rear. He looked at Cesare Marconi.

Marconi looked back. "Go away," he said. "I'm burglarizing Antonio's quarters and don't want to be bothered."

The maggiore quivered but momentarily held his ground.

The relative of the Firenze chief of state said nastily, "I'll get my mother to tell my aunt you were seen talking to an Engelist. *Then* you'll be in the soup, Roberto old friend."

"What Engelist? No member of the Marconi family—even you—would ever tell a deliberate falsehood."

Cesare Marconi leered at him. "Me—that's who. Do you deny you're talking to me, right this minute? An admitted Engelist."

The maggiore was indignant.

Helen said to him helpfully, "You go on. Me an' Gertrude'll keep an eye on him."

Maggiore Verona came to unhappy decision, bowed, muttered, "Signorina, Signori," and left.

The great Marconi looked after him and sneered.

Jerry said to Zorro, "How's the janitor accommodations in the cellar?"

Zorro glowered at him. "Shut up. You're in luck, up here."

109

"I'm always in luck," Jerry said mildly. "And now I'm really in. I get the feeling the First Signore is going to try to sell me the local equivalent of the Brooklyn Bridge."

The Florentine was looking at the two of them.

Horsten quickly changed the subject. "I don't believe I've had the pleasure of meeting you, uh, Mr. Marconi."

Jerry said, to Zorro, as well as to Horsten, "This is the Florentine I told you about. We met this morning at the Florida Café."

"I had guessed. Tell me, Signore Marconi, why didn't the maggiore, just now, challenge you? I thought that on this world challenges were exchanged on the lightest of excuse."

"And run the chance of killing a member of the First Signore's immediate relations?" He had given up his attempt to locate his cousin's favorite potable, and returned with his oversized drink of whiskey to his seat.

"Frankly," Horsten said, "I was somewhat surprised that His Zelenza himself didn't challenge you."

The Florentine was at his full ease. "Doctor—you are Dr. Horsten, of course? You were on Tri-Di, you know. The cameras were on you there at the university with Academician Udine. Doctor, an example is the Old West of the historical fiction Tri-Di shows. Those final scenes, where the two top gunmen come down the main street and shoot it out. It never happened, you know. You must read up on it some time. Very educational. In actuality, men of the Wyatt Earp and Billy the Kid gunman level took full care not to step on each other's toes. Very professional about it. It was much easier to shoot unarmed men down in the O.K. Corral and later brand them rustlers, since you were a marshal and who could say you nay? Or to run up your score of twenty-one notches from ambush, like our famed juvenile delinquent."

Zorro, his handsome face grimacing, said, "What's all this about you being an Engelist? All we hear about on this screw-box world, is the Engelists, but you never see one." The Vacamundo cattleman was absently pounding his tranca in the palm of his left hand.

"Now you have the exception that proves the rule," the Florentine said. "In me, you meet an Engelist."

Jerry said, "Do you mean to say you really think you've got a chance of overthrowing this government? Why, half the population spends its time sniffing out subversives. Look at that cabinet of the First Signore. Ten men and all but one of them working on internal security. Go to

110

the library and ask for a book on Engelism, and they throw you in the jug. Open your mouth about the Engelists, and thirteen bystanders howl for the police."

Cesare Marconi again let his mask slip momentarily, and there was the drawn seriousness. "Signore Rhodes, don't be overly impressed by the efforts governments make to prevent their institutions from being subverted. Social revolution can be equated to the fundamental change involved in an egg becoming a chick. Let us say that there might be some elements who are desirous of having the egg remain an egg. To that end, they may paint the shell of the egg with crosses, angels and cherubs. Or they might paint it red, white and blue, or other patriotic colors of other ages. They might inscribe it with all sorts of speeches and slogans, dreamed up by the most competent speech writers and advertising men available. However, that chick cannot long be put off."

"Gosh," Helen said.

Cesare Marconi looked at her thoughtfully before going on. "So it is with social change. If one is pending—I am not speaking of mere military revolt, or of overthrowing one group of opportunists for the benefit of another, while basic institutions are retained—then those who oppose have their work cut out. You can spend endlessly, paying your educational system from schoolmarms to professors to teach the young why it's no-go. You can subsidize ministers of every denomination to thunder against it in church and synagogue, temple and black mass coven. Alleged great thinkers can write lengthily on why it is against human nature, or whatever, but if it's pending, you'd best have it."

Helen said, in her child's treble, "Or what happens, Mr. Great Martini?"

"*Marconi!*"

"If the little chick doesn't break the shell, huh? What happens?"

He took her in, an edge of bafflement there. "It either breaks the shell, when the breaking is due, Signorina, or it dies."

Jerry said, "How does that fit in with your analogy?"

"In comparison with society? In society, when a social revolution is pending and is put off, then reaction is the inevitable alternative—usually bloody reaction, Signore Rhodes."

The Florentine came to his feet deliberately, and looked about at them. "And now, you must pardon me."

111

Suddenly there was an evil looking, black compact weapon in his hand. Its muzzle swept them, obviously in the grip of a more than ordinarily competent user.

His voice was dangerous now. "I am interested in taking a very thorough look at your luggage, Signori."

There was a flicker in the hand of Zorro Juarez, even as Dorn Horsten snapped, "Zorro, no!"

Too late. A tendril flicked from the end of the tranca. Almost lazily, the speed deceptive, it reached and curled about the small arm. As quickly as it had appeared a split second before in the beautiful quick draw of the Florentine, that quickly the gun vanished from his hand. Magically, it was in the grasp of Zorro Juarez, who was looking mockingly at Cesare Marconi.

That duelist, smiling faintly, put his hands in his pockets and nodded. "That's what I thought," he said.

He looked from Zorro to Dorn Horsten, to Jerry Rhodes, each in their turn. "I didn't know which one it would come from, or how. But I got the impression that when somebody yells, 'stick 'em up' at this little group, it doesn't react exactly as surface appearances might indicate." He looked down at Helen. "I can't figure out where you come in," he said.

Helen stuck her tongue out at him.

He turned and headed for the door.

"Stop!" Zorro snapped, the gun at the ready.

Cesare Marconi took his turn at a mocking grin. "Why?" he said, over his shoulder. "I found out what I came to find out. Now I want to think about it." He twisted his mouth at the threat of the weapon. "You wouldn't dare use that."

"Wait long enough for a question or two," Horsten said, after glaring his disgust at Zorro. "Where did you get the gun?"

"Wondering how I got it past the guards, eh?" Marconi shook his head. "You needn't suspect that I'm a plant they let by with the shooter because we're in cahoots. It was stashed in the bar. My beloved cousin keeps them about his quarters—an assassin complex. I don't blame him."

"Are you really an Engelist?"

The Florentine smiled wryly. After a thoughtful pause, he said, "Yes."

"Why did you hesitate?"

The mouth was still wry. "Perhaps, some day, I'll tell you."

Zorro said to the scientist, "Scop?"

"Shut up."

Cesare Marconi was mocking of voice again. "You're *really* not what you seem, are you?" He looked at Zorro. "So you have truth serum on hand. Naughty, naughty."

Zorro said, "One last question. What do you know about the Dawnworlds?"

Horsten's face froze in disapproval. Jerry Rhodes' eyebrows went up.

For the first time since his arrival, the self-named Great Marconi seemed out of his depth. "Dawnworlds? Never heard of them."

Horsten said, "Evidently, some new planets that might eventually join up with our confederation."

The Florentine scowled his puzzlement at Zorro Juarez, shrugged and turned, saying over his shoulder, "And once again, for the present, Signorina and Signori, farewell."

This time, they made no effort to halt him as he left.

When he was gone, Horsten glared at Zorro. "Have you gone completely around the bend? Didn't you have sense enough not to take his gambit when he pulled that gun? What was the hurry? Any one of us could have taken him, at any time."

"Given luck," Jerry said.

Zorro was embarrassed. "I acted without thinking. Sorry. It makes me nervous, somebody with a shooter in his hand."

Helen snorted, matching her big companion's disgust. "Nervous people don't make good Section G operatives," she said. "But what in the name of the Holy Ultimate was the idea of asking him about the Dawnworlds?"

Zorro flared up defensively. "Damn it, none of you seem to realize that something's off-beat about this Dawnworld thing. You know what one of those over-muscled goons asked, on the way down to that two-by-four room they've boxed me into?"

He had all eyes.

"One of them mentioned the fact that I was from overspace and asked me, in off-hand curiosity, if I'd heard anything new about the Dawnworlds. I tried to draw him out, without saying anything myself, and came up with a rumor he'd heard. Evidently, some outfit, somewhere, is getting together an expedition to raid these Dawnworlds. Not connected with any government, mind you. Some private pirate gang."

"*What!*" Horsten blurted.

Zorro threw up a hand in a gesture of disgust. "All I'm telling you is what I heard. That's why I asked this Marconi character if he knew anything. We've blown our cover with him anyway. We might've learned something."

"One thing," Helen said grudgingly. "I doubt if our Great Marconi is an *agent provocateur*. If he is, then we're in the chowder already. But I don't think he is."

"And I don't think he's an Engelist, either," Jerry said.

Helen looked at him. "Why not?"

Jerry shrugged it off in deprecation. "I don't know. He's got something simmering. What, I don't know. But from everything we've seen and heard, these Engelists are a bunch of crackpots, and I don't get quite that impression about Cesare Marconi."

Dorn Horsten snorted. "If he's an Engelist, it's for the purpose of using them. I'm afraid that friend Marconi is one of the ruling hierarchy of Firenze who's managed to get expelled from the inner ranks, and wants back in."

Jerry said, "Well, I wouldn't be surprised if he made it. Compared to that First Signore, he's a brain."

"Which is more than I can say for you," Helen snarled. "What do you think Dorn was pointing at his watch for? What do you think I said Geneva for?"

Jerry looked at her blankly.

"When you were telling d'Arrezzo about all the supposed capital you've got. Geneva, Geneva. The planet Geneva, where the only industry is interplanetary banking and exchange and making chronometers. If you've got variable capital in large amounts on hand, it'd be stashed safely away on Geneva."

"Oh," Jerry said apologetically. He brightened. "Evidently they've checked out my cover, and found that I'm supposedly loaded with the stuff."

Horsten said, "If Irene Kasansky handled your cover, it's handled, period. She's undoubtedly fed into the records information indicating your family is one of the wealthiest in United Planets."

Jerry lighted up. "There should be some way for me to blow some of it." He added quickly, "Just in the way of maintaining the front, of course."

Zorro growled, "How about buying this damned hotel and putting another floor on it so I can get some decent accommodations?" He looked at Horsten. "Shouldn't we report again to Sid Jakes?"

Helen hopped down from her chair. "If you had your way, we'd report to Jakes every hour, on the hour. Our cover's blown badly enough as it is. We'd better keep that communicator off the sub-space waves as much as we can."

"Well, he ought to know about this new Dawnworld development. Possibly there's something he can add to what we know. Something we can use."

"Our assignment's Firenze," Horsten said. "Let Metaxa and Jakes worry about the Dawnworlds."

Helen had approached the bar and squatted down before it on her heels, in a compelling childlike stance. She looked at the lock of the compartment the First Signore had used earlier. After a moment of contemplation, she took a hairpin from her blonde tresses.

She said, "Hm."

"Hey!" Horsten snapped.

She ignored him. Her tiny hands were, as always, deft. The door opened. Helen peered inside.

"That's what I thought," she said. "Three bottles of the stuff. Tricky miser, isn't he?" She reached into the interior, brought forth a full bottle of the exotic liqueur beloved by the First Signore of Firenze. She held the bottle up and read the label. "Twelve Star Golden Chartreuse," she said. "He hordes it as though he couldn't get another jug of the stuff with all the loot in his treasury."

"Put it back," Horsten said. "He probably couldn't. I've heard of it. There's no more available. When Betelgeuse Three was first explored, it didn't allow colonization. The planetary engineering boys went to work and the biome balance was thrown off. When the first colonists moved in, the berry from which the beverage was made, surprisingly similar to the Earth plant of the ericaceous genus *Vaccinium,* was still surviving, and continued to do so for possibly half a century. During that period, the liqueur was laid down. Supposedly it has the most delicate bouquet and flavor of all time. However, ecology of Betelgeuse Three had been altered to the point where the berry slowly became extinct."

She activated the stopper. "So you can't get any more? You know, the stuff grows on you."

"Put it back, you little lush," Horsten said. "If you can't get any more, why develop a taste for it?"

Helen ignored him. She put the bottle down by her side momentarily, bent back to the keyhole with her hairpin. She locked the small door again, came erect with the bottle, and acquired a glass from the bar.

She went back to the overgrown chair she had claimed as her own, put the bottle and glass on the cocktail table, after pouring herself a respectable portion, made herself comfortable and said, "All right, the meeting will come to order. So far, we've been handling this like a bunch of clowns. We need a plan of action."

She raised her glass to her nose and sniffed. "You know" —she nodded to her supposed father—"you're right. It sure stinks pretty. A little sticky, maybe, but real nice."

XI

Dr. Horsten lumbered along the sidewalk with the great dignity of an Imperial penguin. His right forefinger, which in size resembled a small salami, was in the possession of his little girl who, to match his pace, even though he was but strolling, had devised a combination of trip and skip. Beneath her free arm was tucked a rather oversized doll whose bedraggled hair and every-which-way clothing proclaimed it had seen better days.

The big man seemed to have other, deeper things, on his mind, but he dutifully pointed out various sights as they progressed along the streets of Firenze, capital city of the Free Democratic Commonwealth of Firenze. It was quite a charming sight to their fellow pedestrians who couldn't quite make out the actual words exchanged.

Helen tinkled in her childish treble, albeit softly, "There's another one of the obscenities."

"Shush, damnit, watch your language. Somebody'll hear you." He beamed affectionately down at her.

"Watch your own damn language." She smiled back winningly. "What's the use of going out if every one of their multiple security agencies has at least one man on us, plus, probably, the Engelists to boot?"

"It's a matter of getting the feeling of the town. Watch yourself; our cover is already blown badly enough, you diminutive witch."

"Why, you overgrown ox. I ought to clobber you one. Besides, I've *got* the feeling of this jerk planet. It's a nut factory. Half of them in uniform, the other half look like they're on the kind of rations you get on the Welfare State worlds."

Horsten chuckled benignly, as though the little girl had gotten off a childish bit of bright saying.

"Here's a park," he said. "Suppose we sit for a time and give the poor chaps tagging us an opportunity to rest their feet."

116

They found an unoccupied bench and the little girl bounced up beside her daddy and smoothed her pretty skirt self-consciously. She propped the doll up beside her and smoothed its skirt as well.

She murmured, "Still no beep from Gertrude. Evidently they haven't any great shakes in the way of parabolic mikes, at least not the mobile variety."

"Which surprises me, but then I am continually being surprised on this world. It's not exactly as I had expected it from the little Metaxa told us."

"Let's face it. This is a damned police state."

Horsten grunted discomfort at her words. "But with that all-important difference, Helen. The dream of freedom is there. They are fighting to retain it."

"Retain it? It's already gone. It's been smothered in gobbledygook. Which is often what happens to freedom, inalienable rights and such. It's everybody to his own definition, and the devil take the hindmost."

Horsten said in unhappy doggedness, "It's why we were sent here. They're desperately hanging onto free institutions, in the face of one of the most insidious undergrounds in United Planets."

But Helen was feeling more than usually argumentative, even for Helen. "That word freedom is on the elastic side. Wait'll I think of the classic example I memorized back when I was going to school. It's a dilly." She thought for a moment, pink tongue stuck out the side of her mouth.

"Yeah. Here it is. You need the background. The Spanish conquest of Mexico and the Aztecs. The quotation comes from Francisco de Aguilar, one of Cortes' *Conquistadors*. It goes: 'Sometimes the captain gave us very good talks, leading us to believe that each one of us would be a count or duke and one of the titled; with this he transformed us from lambs to lions, and we went out against that large army without fear or hesitation. . . . We had a courageous captain and soldiers who were determined to die for freedom.'"

In spite of himself, Dorn Horsten had to laugh. He said, "I've got a better one. From the state where my people originated, Texas."

"Texas? I thought you came from some planet with a one point four gravity. Texas? Didn't it used to be a political division back on Mother Earth? The only thing that comes to my mind is an old saying, 'If there had been a back door to the Alamo there wouldn't have been a Texas.'"

117

Horsten winced. "Luckily for you, I am several generations removed from the old sod. At any rate, the area used to belong to Mexico. Immigrants from the southern United States were invited in to help populate it. However, after a couple of decades they revolted, desiring freedom."

"Freedom?"

"Freedom. First, it seems as though the Mexicans, way down in the capital, Mexico City, wanted to tax them as any other Mexicans. But that wasn't the worst abridgment of freedom. It seems as though Mexico had abolished slavery and the newly arrived emigrants weren't allowed the freedom to own slaves. Happily with the aid of 'volunteers' from America, such as Davy Crockett and Jim Bowie, they threw off the Mexican yoke and established a new country whose laws allowed slavery. They applied for entry into the United States and when it was granted submitted to paying the taxes to Washington which they had refused to Mexico City, half the distance away. So the freedom to own slaves was evidently the more germane freedom for which they fought."

Helen snorted. "But, let's get back to freedom here on Firenze. We've got to get cracking, or we're going to pull a zero for poor Lee Chang. And, thus far, we know precious little more about these Engelists than we did when Ross Metaxa briefed us."

"Do you think Zorro and Jerry will be able to make some sort of contact? Frankly, I got exactly nowhere with my local scientists. I could be mistaken, but the impression I got was that none of them belonged to the underground. In fact, none of them seemed interested in the movement, even when I dropped a few hints."

Helen said, "Zorro'll make his contacts today with agricultural elements. Possibly they're more politically minded than your double-domes."

"If he can stop thinking about the Dawnworlds long enough. See here, what do you think about Jerry?"

"What is there to think about Jerry? Lee Chang pulled a blank when she brought that one into her Department of Special Talents."

"I don't know. How do you explain the phenomenon of his luck?"

"It's that damn *morale* of his. That air of knowing perfectly well that everything is going to work out for him. It simply never occurs that it could be otherwise. Suppose you're playing poker. You've got, say, four queens and the pot's gigantic. You look over at him, knowing his reputation for luck. He's got this idiotic confidence on his face. You have inner qualms. Still wearing that complete rejection of the classic poker face, he raises. Now you *know* he's got at least four kings and probably a straight flush. Your own morale shattered, you fold. Actually, what's he probably got is a pair of deuces." She snorted disgust again.

Horsten looked at her. "Suppose you called him instead of folding?"

"You don't. That's what makes you so furious, afterwards. Did you ever play poker with him?"

The big man shuddered. "I wouldn't bet him it was Tuesday, on Tuesday. As a scientist, I don't believe in time travel, and I'd hate to be the one to prove myself wrong."

"Why, Dorn, you old fuddy-duddy. You made a funny."

He suddenly sat erect. "Poker!" he exclaimed.

"What's the matter?"

"Where's Jerry?"

"He was going to wait until the First Signore came back to the suite and go through the pretense of looking into investment opportunities. There's always the off chance that some of these Engelists are in the highest places, among d'Arrezzo's own financial advisers. It wouldn't be the first time a revolt has been sponsored from the top down. Look at Franco, look at Hitler. . . ."

"Poker?" Horsten ejaculated, coming hurriedly to his feet.

"What's the matter with you?"

He grabbed her by the hand and took off in the direction from which they had come. Her short legs had to blur to keep up with his pace.

"Why do you think our friend Antonio d'Arrezzo was so compliant about letting Jerry—and us—remain in his personal suite?"

"He bet with Jerry, and lost! Slow down, damn it!"

He looked desperately up and down the street, even as he hurried. Passersby now looked at them, startled. Gertrude was being dragged along by one leg; Helen's hair streamed back.

"Aren't there any hovercabs in this confounded town!" he complained. "How do you know the First Signore lost that bet?"

She blinked up at him.

"Jerry didn't look. He never looks. He automatically
119

assumes he's won. You didn't see the coin, I didn't. Nobody saw it but d'Arrezzo. Are you sure Jerry won?"

"What are you driving at? Look out!"

Dorn Horsten, in blind hurry to get back to the hotel, had started across a street. A small, two-seat sports hovercar was upon them, its klaxon blurting hysterically.

Horsten straight-armed it with his left, and the hood accordioned in a crash and moan of ruptured metal. Not even bothering to look back, he hustled Helen on.

"Didn't you get those questions about Jerry's supposed resources? What form he has his capital in? And you know what we've briefed Jerry to say."

"What're you *talking* about!" she wailed. Only her acrobatic training was keeping her on her feet and saving her from being dragged by the agitated scientist.

"Large amounts of cash, and Firenze is a planet that's evidently short of negotiable exchange. Jerry supposedly has an almost infinite amount of variable capital deposited on Geneva, famed for its numbered accounts. Famed for the politicians and treasurers who have taken it on the lam from the planets where they held office."

"Oh, oh," Helen said. "He asked Jerry if he knew how to play poker!" She reached up and snagged her companion's belt, hit her heels against the sidewalk and gracefully bounded to the other's shoulder. "Get a move on, horsey!"

No cab was forthcoming and they were forced to retrace the whole way back to the *Albergo Palazzo* on foot. At the main entrance, Dorn Horsten came to a quick halt. The Great Marconi was emerging.

The self-named Engelist beamed at them. "Ah, the celebrated Dr. Horsten. I was just refused entrance to your quarters. But here you are."

"What did you want?"

Cesare Marconi negligently let his eyes go back and forth, checking their vicinity, before saying, "On considering you and your associates at greater length, it occurred to me that we might exchange further information."

The big scientist hesitated. "Look. Come along. Perhaps we could use an extra witness—a Florentine witness."

The other's eyebrows went up, but he trailed along. He murmured, "Very well, but believe me, my most fervent oath to veracity is as though written on expanding gas, in this town."

On the way to the private elevator which led to the

penthouse suite, Marconi said, "And what is the great emergency?"

Helen, still perched on Horsten's shoulder, her arms around his neck, said, "My daddy thinks maybe Mr. First Signore is gonna try and gyp my Uncle Jerry." She added, "He doesn't know my Uncle Jerry."

Cesare Marconi looked at her thoughtfully. He murmured, "And I am afraid your Uncle Jerry doesn't know Cousin Antonio. One does not become a chief executive on any world without certain devious qualities. Certainly, one does not become First Signore without them."

"My Uncle Jerry is lucky," Helen announced.

"So is my cousin Antonio. He's lucky somebody hasn't shot him already. It's high time he got out from under."

They reached the penthouse, to be greeted by a host of the First Signore's bodyguards. The officer in charge scowled at Cesare Marconi. "Signore, I have already informed you that His Zelenza . . ."

Dorn Horsten bit out, "Citizen Marconi accompanies me. I am His Zelenza's guest."

"But the First Signore has ordered that he not be disturbed!"

The small group was hustling past him to the door of the suite. Horsten said, "Don't be an ass, my good fellow. I *live* here."

Helen made a face at the security man.

Inside, they pulled up abruptly. Exactly what Horsten had dreaded finding wasn't clear, but not this.

Space had been cleared for a big table in the living room's center. Two or three of the faceless staff which accompanied the Florentine chief of state were busily at work on it. To one side Jerry Rhodes and their host, Antonio d'Arrezzo, glasses in hand. With them stood a newcomer to the Section G group. He was a smallish man, evidently nervous by nature and with added worries currently besieging him.

The First Signore scowled. "Cesare! I thought I . . ."

Cesare Marconi made his usual sweeping bow. "The good doctor insisted I accompany him."

Horsten looked about the room, even as he lowered Helen to the floor. "What transpires?"

Jerry said, "The First Signore is being kind enough to introduce me to one of his favorite games."

"Poker?" Helen blurted inadvertently. She was ignored.

At that moment, four of the goon guards came staggering in from a rear room. Between them they carried a large and weighty wheel-like object. They manhandled it to the table, heaved together and settled it to one end.

"Roulette!" Horsten said.

"Ah," the First Signore said, turning his attention from his black sheep cousin. "Then you are acquainted with my secret vice, Doctor. I would invite you to participate but I suspect, that as a scientist, you are slightly out of your financial depth. The Signore Rhodes and I, ha ha, have had words. We have challenged each other to play for, ha ha, sizable stakes."

"Ha ha, is right," Helen muttered, meandering off in the direction of the bar, Gertrude slung under her left arm.

Jerry took a pull at the glass he held in his hand. His voice was slightly hazy. He said, "Great opportunity. I was telling His Zellensidor . . ."

The nervous little man standing next to the First Signore looked pained.

". . . about having my capital stashed away on Geneva, an' he pointed out he had a lotta interests here on Firenze such as my mother sent me over to take a look at. 'Ranium mines, and all. So the Tenth Signore, here, just by coincidence, like, turned up. An' he can handle the whole thing. So we're gonna have a friendly game, an' maybe Tony . . ."

The Tenth Signore looked pained again.

". . . maybe Tony'll get some of my negotiable capital, or maybe I'll get some of his securities."

Horsten said quickly, "But, Jerry, have you considered all this? Your mother and all. Are you sure it's fair? That is . . ."

Jerry waved the hand in which he held the glass, spilling only a few drops. "Oh, I warned 'em. Didn't I, Tony? Told him I was lucky."

The First Signore beamed over his shoulder at Horsten. He was supervising the final setting-up of the roulette layout. "I, too, am inordinately fortunate," he told the scientist.

Horsten looked at the small confederate of the First Signore. He said, "If I understand it, you carry the Treasury portfolio in His Zelenza's government."

The other bobbed. "That is correct, Signore."

"So I suppose that if your chief is the fortunate one, you can deposit his winnings to a numbered account on Geneva."

Cesare Marconi said mockingly, "Why, Antonio, aren't you ashamed?"

His cousin straightened and turned in anger. "Who let you in, Cesare? I warn you . . ."

Horsten said, giving up trying to convey unspoken messages to his young colleague, "I brought him along, Your Zelenza. Aside from you and your staff, Citizen Marconi is about the only Florentine we have met since setting down on the planet. I was in hopes he could tell me something of the workings of this rather, if you'll pardon me, unexampled world."

The Florentine leader said coldly, "I am afraid his ramblings will avail you little in that regard, Doctor." The roulette table was now operative. He snapped his fingers at the half dozen aides and guards present and they scrambled.

"Well, well." The First Signore rubbed his palms together briskly. "Who shall take the bank?"

Jerry Rhodes finished his drink, but his expression was blank. "Remember, I've never played."

Horsten said, "The percentage is with the bank, Jerry." He was ignored.

The First Signore took the younger man's glass from his hand and turned to the bar. He began to refresh the drink. Inadvertently, his eyes went to the bottle from which he himself, had been drinking. He frowned slightly in puzzlement, put Jerry's glass down and took up the bottle of Golden Chatreuse. He held it to the light, checking its level. He shook his head in bewildered disbelief, but then gave up his trend of thought and went back to mixing another portion for his guest, from a different bottle.

"Doctor," he said. "A beverage for you, as well?" And, grudgingly, "Cesare, since you are here, if I will it or not . . ."

"I'll make my own," the Great Marconi said, and then, twisting the knife in the wound, "I have a predilection for that Betelgeuse drink of yours. I mix it with gingerbeer and sugar."

The First Signore repressed a groan of pure soul agony but returned with the tall glass to Jerry.

He stood in the croupier's place at the head of the table and explained the game. "We have, here, this wheel and little ball. I spin the wheel and toss the ball in. There are thirty-eight slots, in all, into which it may fall; thirty-six of them numbers, one a zero, and one a double zero. Now then, on the table we have places to bet. One for each slot. If you bet on number eighteen, let us say, and

123

the little ball drops into that slot"—he oozed charm—"then you win thirty-six times your bet."

"Wow," Jerry said. "Now, that's something. None of this one-to-one wager. Thirty-six times what you bet. How can you lose? Fascinatin'."

Antonio d'Arrezzo cleared his throat unctuously. "You can lose if the little ball drops into some other slot. Now, there are several other ways in which you can wager. For instance, you will note that half the numbers are red, and half black."

Marconi and Horsten, both sighing, though through different motivation, drifted over to the bar. The Great Marconi took over the job of making them drinks, pouring them fron the bottle of Golden Chartreuse. Its bouquet suffused the immediate vicinity.

"Do you really mix gingerbeer with this stuff?" Horsten said.

"No. I'm just trying to give Antonio ulcers thinking about it. See here, can that friend of yours afford to lose?"

"He could sign a draft on any bank on Geneva to the extent of a billion interplanetary credits, and it wouldn't faze him."

The Great Marconi whistled softly. "Why didn't I see him first?"

Horsten said, "But he's not going to lose. Can your cousin afford a financial jolting?"

"Theoretically, as First Signore, he has in his name the possession of all nationalized industry on Firenze. Theoretically he could sign over their ownership."

"What do you mean, theoretically?"

"Under interplanetary law, his signature would stand up in the Department of Interplanetary Trade on Mother Earth."

"But . . ." Horsten prompted.

Cesare Marconi looked at him. "Isn't it obvious? If he signed away, in his position as chief of state, the public property, his neck would be in a noose before the day was out."

Then why take the chance?"

The Great Marconi pulled at his glass glumly. "He's not going to lose."

The two, carrying their drinks, made their way back to the roulette table. The First Signore had just finished explaining the workings of the ages-old game. Jerry Rhodes stood at the table side, a stack of chips before him. Evidently, through the Tenth Signore, the two contestants had made some sort of financial arrangement so that they could wager.

Jerry took a sip from his glass, set it down and took up a chip. "We'll start off slow," he said, his voice slurring only slightly. "Hundred thousand interplanetary credits on the very number you mentioned—eighteen."

"A . . . hundred . . . thousand . . . interplanetarry . . . credits," Cesare Marconi said.

Dorn Horsten had given up.

Antonio d'Arrezzo spun the wheel. He tossed the plastic ball so that it rolled, counter to the direction of the spin, about the edge of the bowl in which the wheel sat. All eyes were fascinated.

The ball lost momentum, slipped from the rim, hit into the numbered slots, bounced out, bounced in again, seemed to have found its place in slot number thirty, but then gave one last feeble bounce.

"Eighteen!" Jerry blurted happily.

The First Signore stared disbelief.

"Thirty-six to one," Jerry said, grinning around at the small circle of them. "Tha's what I call odds." He looked to the Firenze strong-arm, pinch-hitting as croupier. "Let her roll."

It was the jittery Tenth Signore who said, "Let her roll?"

Jerry Rhodes looked at the Florentine chief of state accusingly. "You said no limit, didn't you?"

"Eh?" Antonio d'Arrezzo was still staring at the plastic ball, nestled in slot eighteen. "Oh. No limit. Why . . . yes, of course." He had been in the process of shoving two stacks of chips, eighteen to the stack, in Jerry's direction, with his croupier stick.

Jerry pushed them all over onto number eighteen.

Cesare Marconi shot Horsten an incredulous look. "You mean he's going to wager thirty-seven hundred thousand interplanetary credits on one spin of the wheel? One chance in thirty-eight of it coming up?"

Horsten shook his massive head. "I told you he was lucky."

"Nobody's that lucky."

The First Signore plucked the ball from the eighteen slot and looked at it. He hefted it. He seemed to shrug infinitesimally, then spun the wheel again. He tossed the ball as he had before.

Jerry said, "A bet of thirty-seven hundred thousand credits at odds of thirty-six to one. Why, I'd have to figure

125

it out. Mother'll be pleased. Mounts to a sizable chunk of that 'ranium industry. We'll go to work on transportation, next." He looked at the Tenth Signore. "Didn't you say that was one of the nationalized industries?"

"Yes."

Cesare Marconi glowered a look of disgust at the young man, turned and went back to refresh his glass. But he had returned by the time the ball was bouncing from slot to slot.

"Eighteen!" Jerry chortled. He looked at Dorn Horsten, as though soliciting approval. "Now isn't that luck?" He turned his shining face to the Florentine Minister of Treasury. "How much of the 'ranium industry do I have now?"

"You own it," the Tenth Signore moaned.

"Now look here . . ." Horsten began, and was completely ignored.

Jerry said, in a burst of enthusiasm, "Let 'er ride again!"

The First Signore shook his head. "But . . . but if you won again, I wouldn't have the chips to . . . to pay off."

Jerry upended his drink, tossed the empty glass over his shoulder. "Chips, snips," he slurred. "All or nothin'. One more rolla the wheel. If it comes up eighteen, you lose. Everything. I own all the nationalized industry on Firenze."

For long moments, silence reigned. The First Signore was breathing deeply. So deeply that he sounded as though he had but finished the climbing of a considerable peak.

"*Your Zelenza!*" The Tenth Signore groaned.

"Quiet!" d'Arrezzo ground out. He turned to his opponent and whispered, "You're on."

He picked up the plastic ball, stared at it for a long moment, hefted it slightly. He shook his head, and spun the wheel.

There was commotion at the entry. The door banged open.

The First Signore looked up to glare.

Zorro, in the hands of two of the brawniest of the Florentine guards, was being dragged along, in the trail of a gaudily uniformed officer of what the Section G representatives now recognized as the Ministry of Anti-Subversion. The officer held something in his right hand, and there was an air of triumph in his every move.

"What is the meaning of this!" d'Arrezzo barked.

"Your Zelenza!" the newcomer returned, completely uncowed. "They're subversive spies! All spies. We captured this one sending a report to his superiors back on Earth.

We were able to tape most of it." He held up that which he had been carrying in his hand.

"Hey!" Helen bleated from across the room where she had retreated with her doll. "That's my Gertrude's Tri-Di Dolly Set. You give me that back!"

It was a good try, but without any response whatsoever.

"Report?" the First Signore snapped. His glare encompassed the otherworldlings.

"Yes, Your Zelenza. Most of it is unintelligible. Something about Dawnworld planets. However, we have enough to prove that these"—with a sweeping hand he indicated Jerry, the disgruntled Zorro and Dorn Horsten—"are all operatives of Section G, evidently some espionage agency of the Octagon."

"I see," the First Signore said.

Helen had come up to take her stance next to Horsten, at the roulette table, her doll under her arm.

Gertrude began to go, *Beep, beep, beep.*

XII

THE SOUND was audible enough for all to hear. The Florentines were not the only ones to scowl.

Of a sudden, Dorn Horsten moved. He took two lumbering steps, grasped hold of the gigantic roulette wheel, and heaved. It came up in his huge hands, and he rested it on one side on the floor. As all watched, taken aback, he pulled away the metal sheathing which covered the bottom. Beneath was a bed of wires and miniature power packs.

"Ah ha," the doctor snorted.

Cesare Marconi whinnied amusement. "Why Cousin Antonio, a rigged wheel? No wonder you were surprised when you didn't win, and no wonder you won so often before at your parties to raise campaign funds."

But the First Signore, in his rage, was having none. He whirled on Jerry Rhodes, now completely sober.

"An agent of Section G! I have heard rumors of this Section G and its subverting of member worlds of the United Planets. All a farce! You have no unlimited wealth on Geneva. You would have cheated me!"

"Ha!" Helen snorted. "Look who's talking."

The open palm of Antonio d'Arrezzo lashed out across the face of the younger man. Jerry Rhodes, off guard, staggered back.

"We will meet on the field of honor!" the First Signore snapped. "Name your weapon!" He turned his glare on the scientist and then went on to Zorro Juarez. "And when I have finished with this make-believe interplanetary tycoon, then you, and you!"

The Firenze chief of state turned his glare on Cesare Marconi. "And then, perhaps you. I am not amused by you befriending these enemies of the State, nor, for that matter your professed adherence to the Engelists." He turned back to Jerry, still fuming. "Your choice of weapons, Signore." The term "signore" came out a sneer.

Jerry blinked at him, still not quite accommodated to the last few moments of developments.

"Uh, Sten guns," he said. "Sten guns at five paces."

Antonio d'Arrezzo whirled to his guard officer. "He has chosen. Make immediate arrangements!" Stiff-legged, he strode for the entry and the doorway, the Tenth Signore bustling along behind him.

The suite had emptied save for the Section G operatives and Cesare Marconi. The latter was eyeing Jerry Rhodes laconically. He turned to the bar, began making himself another drink with his cousin's precious Betelgeuse Chartreuse. "What," he said, "is a Sten gun?"

Jerry, rubbing his face where he had been slapped, in the classical challenge to duel, laughed in self-deprecation. "That'll stop him," he said.

Zorro, Helen and Horsten all looked at him, even as they gathered themselves.

He said, in rueful explanation, "I took a page from the Doc's book, when that university scientist challenged him. I named an impossible weapon."

Marconi bent an eye on him, even as he poured. "Impossible?"

Jerry allowed himself a chuckle. "A Sten gun. I saw one in a Tri-Di historical show once. Second or Third World War, back on Earth. Anyway, they used to drop them to the partisans behind the lines. Very simply constructed submachine gun."

The Florentine said, in interest, "What's impossible about it?"

Jerry scowled. "Why, it's almost as ancient as Dorn's Macedonian pike. There are no such things any more."

Cesare Marconi looked at him. "I have unfortunate news for you. Way-out weapons are quite a fad on the Firenze field of honor. There is an amazingly complete

128

library on them in the archives of the College of the Code Duello."

Zorro said, speaking for the first time since he had been hauled so unceremoniously into the room. "You mean they'd make up a couple, to order, just for this one duel?"

"Yes. In practically no time at all."

Jerry flinched. "But . . . but the ammunition, and so forth."

"They'll make that too. Do you know what a Sten gun fires?"

"I . . . I think they fire bullets. A clip of twenty or so."

"At five paces?" the Florentine said. "Holy Ultimate, you'll both be hamburger. No, only you. I have no great respect for my highly placed cousin, but he has perhaps the fastest reflexes on the planet Firenze. It is no mistake he is the First Signore."

Helen said, "Look. While you're over there, make me one of those king-size drinks too, will you?"

They used the heavy table, which a few moments past had been utilized for the roulette layout, for their conference. The wheel lay to one side, where Dorn Horsten had let it drop upon revealing its crooked nature. Zorro had swept the felt layout board to the floor as well, and all had brought up seats, save Helen who remained in the comfort chair she had made her own.

Cesare Marconi, somehow, had automatically become a member of the group. He said to Dorn Horsten, "What's this Section G? My friend, Bulchand, just before he was killed in a put-up duel, revealed he belonged to it, and that undoubtedly new representatives would be coming to replace him from Earth, if he was killed. It's why I contacted you. You seemed unlikely, but you were the only travelers from Earth in some time."

The scientist looked at him quizzically. Finally, he said, "All I can tell you is that its purpose, so far as Firenze is concerned, is to get this planet back on the road to progress."

"That sounds good enough to me."

Helen said, "I'm beginning to think I know the answer to this already, but just for the record, if you're in favor of progress on Firenze, what're you doing in the ranks of the Engelists?"

Marconi eyed her in speculation. "I'm beginning to think I know the answer to this question already, too, but you're an adult, aren't you?"

Helen snorted and looked at Zorro and Jerry. "Evidently more so than my two colleagues, here." She looked Marconi full in the face. "What're you doing in the ranks of the Engelists?"

"*Ranks* of the Engelists? I *am* the Engelists."

Dorn Horsten was scowling at him. "What in the name of the Holy Ultimate is that supposed to mean?"

Helen looked at her large partner. "Isn't it obvious? What he's saying is, there are no Engelists on this crackpot planet. There are none, never were any." A speculative look came to her face. "I was about to add, and never will be."

"Nothing's making sense around here!" Zorro complained. "What do you mean, there are no Engelists? We were sent here, all the way from Earth to . . ."

Helen overrode him. "Get stute, love. It's all phony. The powers that be on this zany world maintain themselves with a police state camouflaged as a democratic regime that has to curtail all liberties, civil and otherwise, in the supposed fight against subversion. It's not the first time witch hunting has been resorted to, when there were precious few witches, in order to maintain the status quo. This is just the most complete example known in history."

Jerry said, "You mean everybody on Firenze spends practically all their time looking for subversives that aren't there? How about that leaflet Maggiore Verona showed us?"

Horsten grunted. "Obviously, the government itself printed them up. Which explains how stupidly it was worded. No, Helen's right. It's a sort of reverse of the old Roman adage. When confronted with possible revolt from your people at home, stir up trouble abroad. In this case, the powers that be pretend the need to unite the country against subversives when their real interest is to preserve themselves in control. Only those on the very highest levels are in on the secret. Not even that colonel in the Anti-Subversion Ministry, whom Helen and I interrogated, knew the real situation."

Zorro growled, "What gets me is that when you arrive at the top, the First Signore—not to mention that silly little member of his council, the Tenth Signore—you draw a small-time crook, and not a particularly smart one, at that."

Dorn Horsten said, "That's one of the mistakes the man in the street has made down through the ages. He simply can't realize that those in ultimate power are not, necessarily, competent to exercise power. And that applies to the most highly evolved societies as well as the backward." He snorted. "Take the first caesars, following the founders of the Empire, Julius and Augustus. From Tiberius, through Caligula and Claudius to Nero. Sex deviates, sadistic monsters, playboys, mass murderers. Caligula was actually quite mad. The end of the Julian line? Nero, who fiddled around until the Empire burned and they were heading to lynch him when he committed suicide.

"It's not the only example. History teems with them. But can you imagine some sincere Centurion, stationed at an important outpost on the Parthian frontier, being told that the God-Emperor, back in Rome, had made one of his racehorses a Consul, and made prostitutes of his two sisters? He simply wouldn't have, couldn't have, believed it. You don't have to go that far back. Would a good British subject of the early Nineteenth Century have believed you, had you told him his monarchy was crazy? Did the American people of the Twentieth Century have an idea, really, of the true competence of some of their elected presidents?"

Jerry said, "But this isn't just a matter of an incompetent getting to power. Sure, that's happened before, especially when rulers inherited their jobs, but even when they could get elected to them because they happened to have a photogenic face for TV, or oozed sincerity, politician style. But this whole government, the whole planet, is a farce."

Helen sighed. "It's not the first time there, either. Remember some of the supposed sovereign states, back before man reached into space. What was the one on the French Riviera? Monaco. A bit over three hundred acres. Half the size of Central Park, in the New York City of the time. But it had a supposed prince, princess and all the rest of the feudalistic foofaraw. Even that wasn't the most ludicrous. Did you ever hear of the Sovereign Order of the Knights of Malta, which was contemporary with Monaco, the United States and the rest? It was a sovereign country with its own citizens, ambassadors, air force, license plates and so forth and it occupied the second floor of a villa in Rome, as its sole territory."

She changed the subject. "All right. Fine. Ross Metaxa, back in the Octagon, was sold a bill of goods, along with everyone else. There are no Engelists on Firenze and the present ruling class are incompetents, not patriots fighting an underground. But we've got more pressing problems."

She looked at Zorro. "How in *hell* did you get caught by those dimwits?"

The dark complected Vacamundian was surly. "I don't know. It didn't occur to me that they'd have that cubicle of a room, occupied by a junior janitor, bugged. I thought the rest of you were wrong, that we ought to report on these Dawnworld developments, so I took your disguised communicator and called Sid Jakes. You know the rest."

"No use crying over spilled milk," Jerry Rhodes said.

All eyes went to him.

Helen snarled, "I ought to spill some milk over you. What was the idea of getting into that stupid roulette game with the big shot? You knew damn well you didn't have any real negotiable credits on Geneva."

Jerry was plaintive. "I couldn't escape him. I couldn't have got out of it without blowing our cover. He was hot to get his hands on hard exchange in a numbered account on Geneva, and he wasn't going to take no."

Helen looked at Cesare Marconi, who had been absorbing it all, his face intelligently serious. "Why don't you start talking?" she said.

He nodded. "Obviously, my cousin was trying to get out from under while he still had his skin. He probably does not wish to go through even this next pseudo-election."

"Why not?" Zorro said.

Marconi turned to him. "During the elections, the First Signore's immunity to challenge no long applies, at least in so far as other potential candidates within the ranks of the Machiavellian Party are concerned. Over the years, a man's reflexes fall off. This is Antonio's second term and he's possibly afraid he wouldn't live to serve another." He looed around at the others. "I can only be ashamed of the fantastically ridiculous institutions of my planet, that the Code Duello should play such a major part. It would seem impossible."

Horsten said, "It's not as unprecedented as all that. We were talking about the United States a moment ago. In its early days, two of its most prominent statesmen, both of presidential caliber, fought a duel. Alexander Hamilton and Aaron Burr. One was killed, the other's career was ruined by the results of the fight."

"At any rate," Marconi said, "Antonio's problems are probably solved. He'll have his Anti-Subversion lads do up a good case against you. The fact that you're from overspace makes it still better. This duel will be highly popular and"—he looked at Jerry glumly—"his killing you will undoubtedly result in his retaining his office. He'll be so popular that his opponents wouldn't dream of opposing him openly." His eyes went to Horsten and Zorro. "Then, he'll take on you two, just to parlay his popularity to the skies."

Jerry cleared his throat. "Suppose I finish him, instead. I'm kind of lucky."

The Florentine shook his head. "Luck isn't going to be involved. And, you being a subversive from overspace, if by the wildest chance you did win, the mob would find you and pull you down. If you're lucky, there'll be a quick death under Antonio's fire, which is what will happen anyway. As I told you, his reflexes are admirable, possibly next to my own, the best on Firenze."

Zorro said, "If you're so good, why aren't you First Signore?"

Marconi looked at him and said very slowly, "I told you I was the sole Engelist on Firenze. I am opposed to the present institutions. And that includes dueling as a method of achieving political ends." He snorted self-deprecation. "In spite of the fact that events have made it necessary for me to take up tutoring fencing to make my living."

Helen popped up from her chair and strode over to the bar, the childish skip gone from her walk. She grabbed up the sole remaining bottle of Golden Chartreuse and returned with it to the table to pour herself a healthy slug. "What an aroma," she murmured.

And then, "Look. We're going around and around, getting nowhere. By the looks of it, we're being kept in this suite until the slaughter. Jerry's going to have his work cut out avoiding that appointment in the Parco Duello. And . . ."

"Not in the park," Cesare Marconi said, shaking his head. "Too big an event. It'll be in the auditorium of the College of the Code Duello, where the Tri-Di coverage will be perfect."

Jerry said, "You mean this whole thing goes on the air?"

"Like I said, Signore Rhodes, it will be the making of the First Signore in this pseudo-election. It will be played up to the point where every man, woman and child on Firenze will be glued to the Tri-Di set."

"Hm," Helen said.

The Great Marconi reached out for the bottle of Chartreuse, but little Helen was before him. She snatched the rare liqueur. There was only an inch or so left.

The Florentine's eyebrows went up. She didn't look particularly the worse for wear, in spite of the hefty number of drinks she had poured down since the First Signore and his party had left.

Helen said, "I think I've got a use for this."

Dorn Horsten grunted. "You've had a use for all three bottles the bar originally was equipped with," he said. "I'll never get over it. You put away alcohol like it was strained fruit juice."

"Shut up, you big lummox. I'm thinking."

Horsten grunted again and turned back to the Florentine duelist. "To get back to Jerry and his rendezvous with your cousin. What will be the procedure?"

"I suppose you two, you and Zorro, will have to be Signore Rhodes' seconds. However, I'll act as your adviser. The manufacturing of the Sten guns shouldn't take more than twenty-four hours. Undoubtedly, Antonio's seconds will then turn up and a time will be set for the meeting. You have, perhaps, a day and a half, at most, two."

Helen said, "No way of escaping? Getting off the planet?"

He looked at her glumly. "With the security forces on this world? And only one spaceport? And with no United Planets Embassy, even? Why do you bother to ask?"

The auditorium of the College of the Code Duello was done up in such wise that it might have been recognized by a showman of yesteryear as a movie set portraying the Florence of the days of the Medici. Perhaps a cinema producer of the past might have so recognized it, though the doubt is there that Michelangelo, Leonardo da Vinci, Raphael, or Donatello would have. Alas, long millennia had expired between the golden Renaissance city and the interior decorators employed by the Machiavellian Party.

Nevertheless, the setting was impressive in its rich grandeur. On the face of it, the First Signore was going to milk every drop of propaganda value from his revenge on the subversives from overspace who had come to undermine the institutions of the Free Democratic Commonwealth of Firenze. Or, so at least had the mass media of the planet announced.

Uniforms were impressive; even those of the enlisted men of the guard were a blaze of color. Officers and high rankers of the immediate staffs of the First Signore and his

Council on Signori were quite breathtaking in their grandeur.

Even Cesare Marconi, for once, had risen above his usual seedy attire and had blossomed forth in the garb of a Florentine of the highest position.

He stood, most unhappily, with the group of Section G operatives in the corner of the auditorium where the protocol officers had assigned them. There were two or three Tri-Di cameras trained on them, otherwise they were free to their own devices.

The self-styled Great Marconi grunted deprecation. "I am beginning to wonder why I am here," he said. "Foot-dragging opposition to my cousin's government is one thing. In the past, nobody took me very seriously. This is another thing."

Zorro said sourly, "What happens now?" ·

"We're waiting for the First Signore. His public relations people undoubtedly have it all figured out. Just the point where suspense has built up to the ultimate, but not quite to where the patriotic citizenry is beginning to weary of the delay. Only the blind, on Firenze, are not watching this, and they're listening."

Helen, now that their cover was irretrievably blown, had improvised from her wardrobe the nearest thing she could achieve to adult wear and a touch of cosmetics. She had rearranged her hair, managed a bit here, a bit there, so that she now appeared to be an adult, albeit a tiny one by the standards of any member of the United Planets save her own world.

Jerry said, not nearly so glum as the occasion might have warranted, "I've always been kind of lucky."

They ignored that.

Dorn Horsten, pushing his glasses back on his nose in irritation, said, "I'm beginning to build up a disregard for your cousin, my friend."

Cesare looked at him. "Don't let your hopes get too high. Antonio will never meet you with Macedonian pikes, nor anything else where your strength might be a factor. Believe me, some way will be found in which his own chances are minimal."

Horsten said, "You mean he'll stack the deck? He doesn't seem to have done so in Jerry's case. Except for his alleged fast reflexes, the duel seems to be fifty-fifty."

"Seems is correct," Cesare said. "I don't trust him."

"But we all inspected and tried out the two weapons before they were sealed in that carrying case, last night."

135

The scientist looked at Jerry in compassion. "You certainly picked the most deadly short-range weapon come down through history."

Zorro said abruptly to their Florentine companion, "Look, isn't there any way for the rest of us to get out of this? It's bad enough that Jerry, here, has obviously had it, but . . ."

"Shut up, lover," Helen snorted.

He glared at her darkly. "We don't win any prizes by going down in noble defeat. If there's anything we can do to help Jerry, very well. But if we can't, our job is to survive and carry on the work. Maybe Marconi has some place we could hide."

But Cesare Marconi was shaking his head. "Forget about it, Juarez. I'm possibly the most observed man on Firenze. They haven't cracked down on me in the past, because of my family connections, but, as Antonio said the last time we saw him, they aren't amused by my professions of being an Engelist. They know that I know the whole thing is a fraud, that there are no Engelists. I couldn't hide you. I couldn't even hide myself."

"There must be some way we can get out from under," Zorro said.

There was a blare of anachronistic clarions.

There was a great animation at the opposite end of the hall, a great stirring. All, save the Section G operatives and their single Florentine adherent, came to formal attention.

Down the center of the auditorium, stiff-legged, the stride of the cavalryman long used to high military boots, came Antonio Cesare Bartolemo d'Arrezzo, First Signore of the Free Democratic Commonwealth of Firenze. He looked to neither left nor right at the perfectly aligned men at arms who flanked his march. In that multitude of the uniformed, his was the simplest garb of all, a simple black duelist's costume, the shirt open at the neck, rubber-soled sport shoes on his feet.

Immediately behind him were his seconds, Alberto Scialanga, the Third Signore, and another high ranking officer, unknown to the otherworldlings until the formalities of the meeting had been gone through.

Cesare Marconi cleared his throat, an element of apology there. "All right," he said. "Here we go. We advance to within five paces, the stipulated distance. Jerry, you stop at that point. Dorn and Zorro, you advance to make last preparations with his seconds, and to receive Jerry's weapon. We went over the details last night. I'll be immediaately behind you, as adviser, in case you have questions."

Helen said, "I don't know what the rules are, but I'm coming along."

Cesare Marconi scowled down at her, began to say something, shook his head, and closed his mouth.

They marched out to meet the First Signore and his people.

Jerry Rhodes' opponent stood there, five correct paces away, his black-clad legs slightly parted, his hands behind his back. His two seconds approached. Dorn Horsten and Zorro Juarez met them halfway, Marconi immediately to their rear. The Third Signore carried an elaborately decorated flat box, the other second a golden key with which he ceremoniously unlocked the container.

Inside were two Sten guns. On the handle of one, in gold inlay, was lettered SIGNORE RHODES, on the other, SIGNORE D'ARREZZO.

The box was extended to Dorn Horsten, who took forth Jerry's weapon and returned with it to his principle.

"Are there any questions, Signori?" Alberto Scialanga said to Horsten and Zorro.

"None," the scientist said unhappily.

The First Signore's men returned to him and proffered the box. He took forth his own weapon, balanced it in his hands as though he had handled such a gun all his life.

A highly decorated officer, the judge, stepped forward. As he did, guards and witnesses shifted out of the line of fire.

He said, his voice loud and clear for the sake of the Tri-Di technicians who were zeroed-in on the scene: "The Signori are familiar with the agreed procedure. Both Signori will turn their backs to each other. I shall count three. On the last, the Signori shall turn and fire at will. Is all understood?"

The First Signore bit out, "Yes."

Jerry said, "I guess so." He looked down at the Sten gun, as though he had never seen a firearm before and had never truly expected to.

All except the two duelists cleared away.

"This is murder," Zorro muttered.

Dorn Horsten looked at him. "We'll have a chance, later," he growled in frustration.

The judge began: "One . . . Two . . ."

All in that great auditorium took deep breath.

"Three!"

The First Signore blurred into a spinning crouch, the Sten gun up at waist level, the finger on the trigger already exerting pressure.

A strange expression washed over his face. His eyes had been on the more slowly turning Jerry Rhodes, but now they shot down to his weapon, unbelievingly. His finger tensed again, in a jerky movement this time.

Jerry had brought his own weapon up, his eyes blinking rapidly. His own finger tensed.

The liquid that jetted from the barrel of Jerry's vicious looking gun hit the ultimate head of Firenze full in the face. It was a yellowish, thickish liquid and inclined to drip and ooze, rather than splatter.

A delicious aroma began to permeate the vicinity.

The visage of Antonio d'Arrezzo fell in complete bewilderment. He shook his head. He stared down at his gun. His eyes, in bewildered shock, registered utter disbelief. His tongue inadvertently came out and licked around his slack, twitching mouth. One hand came up, two fingers touched his moisture bespattered face; he brought them away, stared at them, brought the fingers to his mouth.

It was the judge who giggled first.

But it was the Third Signore who first began to guffaw.

Aftermath

"Luck!" Helen snarled at Jerry Rhodes.

"Why, sure," Jerry said. "Who ever heard of such luck?"

"Luck!" she all but screamed. "It took me half the night to get into that damned room where they had those guns stashed in that supposedly locked box. It must have taken me an hour to pick that lock. And what did I find? They'd got there first and extracted the firing pin from your Sten gun. It took me another hour to figure out how to field strip those confounded primitive shooters, and switch matters around so it was *his* firing pin that was missing, and the necessary parts of my toy water pistol installed in yours, loaded with Chartreuse. And you call it luck!"

"Well," Jerry said placatingly. "That's what I mean. It sure was lucky for me you did all that."

"Oh, shut up!" she snarled. She turned back to where Dorn Horsten had his massive body hunched over the Section G communicator. The faces of both Sid Jakes and

Lee Chang Chu were in the screen, both of them a little on the wide-eyed side.

Horsten was summing it up.

". . . and obviously a farce is what the First Signore and his gang could stand the least, especially on the eve of this pseudo-election of theirs. Nothing will come of it this time, perhaps, but by the next election, if not sooner, Cesare Marconi and his people will have their chance."

"What people?" Sid Jakes demanded. "I thought you said he was the only Engelist on the whole planet."

"Well," Dorn Horsten explained plausibly, "that's why we're going to have to stay on for awhile. We were sent to end the Engelist movement on this planet. But, actually, we're going to have to get it underway. A real underground movement, that is."

Lee Chang Chu murmured, "Talk about Special Talent!"

They sat around, still later, in the living room of the penthouse suite of the First Signore and worked out their situation, over drinks.

They were, it was decided, safe for the immediate future. Antonio d'Arrezzo and his group wouldn't dare molest them, right at present. The full shockwaves of the disaster to the dignity of the First Signore would have to subside before he could so much as show his face. The ludicrous qualities of a regime, a political system, so dependent upon the antique code of the duelist were obviously too prominent in the minds of every thinking person on the planet, right now.

They batted it back and forth and made tentative plans for their activities in support of Cesare Marconi and his organization in embryo.

After a half hour of this, Helen said abruptly, "And now I think it's time for a little game of Truth and Consequences."

"What're you talking about?" Jerry said. "Besides, that game's called Truth *or* Consequences."

"That's what you think, lover," Helen said. "You see these drinks I served you? I put the last of my supply of Scop in them."

Zorro began to come to his feet, his face dark.

But it was then they all noticed that Helen had a very small gun in her chubby right hand and that her eyes were dangerous.

They were—Zorro Juarez, Jerry Rhodes, Dorn Horsten—

familiar enough with the character of the diminutive Helen, so that when she snapped, "Subside, lovers," they subsided and awaited developments.

It was to the big scientist that she turned.

"All right," she said. "Listen, you lummox. In this Section G masquerade we play, do you picture yourself as sort of a romantic, dashing D'Artagnon, Three Musketeers type?"

He tried to hold his teeth firmly clamped. An absolute flare of red started up from his collar, but the word came out.

"Yes."

She laughed sneeringly at him. "You overgrown romantic elephant."

Her eyes went to Jerry. "All right, that was just a test to see if the Scop was working. Now then, this luck of yours. How does it happen? How do you account for it?"

His expression was blank, beyond the effects of the drug. Before he could answer, however, she had snapped, "Keep your hand away from that tranca of yours, Zorro." She looked back at Jerry. "Why?"

"Why—why, it's just luck."

She nodded satisfaction. "I'm glad you didn't know that you've been a parasite on your fellow man by utilizing something more than luck. At least, you're basically honest."

The effects of the drug weren't such as to attack lucidity. Horsten growled, "What does that mean?"

Helen snorted. "You're supposed to be the double-dome of the team. Haven't you figured it out? Our boy, here, evidently has all the psi abilities in the book working for him subconsciously. Everything from telekinesis, when he's flipping that coin of his, or lousing-up even rigged roulette wheels, to telepathy and clairvoyance. For all I know, he even exercises a bit of precognition." She snorted again. "All subconscious, evidently. But from what little I know about it, that's the way psi has often manifested itself down through the ages. Go back far enough and you'll find psi adepts thinking themselves witches, or mediums, or some such."

But now the gun was full on the chest of Zorro Juarez.

"And now we get to the real point. Keep your hands away from that tranca, lover. It's your turn. Why did you join Section G?"

His hands, both on the table top, clinched until fingernails dug into palms. A trickle of sweat found its way down the side of his cheek from the sideburn of his hair.

The gun remained steady and Helen said, her voice empty and cold, "Answer."

"To . . . to . . . learn . . . more . . . about . . . the Dawnworlds."

"Why did you want to learn more about the Dawnworlds?"

His breath was short, desperate. "I . . . I belong . . . to a syndicate . . . that plans to . . . locate . . . the Dawnworlds . . . and secure some . . . of their . . . advanced devices." The shoulders of the man had slumped in defeat.

"Then all of this gobbledygook you've been giving us about local interest in the subject was simply an effort to pry more information from us, and from Sid Jakes?"

"Yes."

The diminutive agent looked at him in disgust. "Lover, you're first going to give us all the dope you possess on this syndicate of yours. Undoubtedly, they're the ones that stole Ronny Bronston's starchart, after you tipped them off to its existence. Sid and Lee Chang can deal with them. And then you're going to get a dose of memory-wash so strong you'll not only forget everything you know about Section G, you'll have to go back to grammar school."